D0342645

BARTLETT'S
SHAKESPEARE
QUOTATIONS

BARTLETT'S
SHAKESPEARE
QUOTATIONS

John Bartlett
Foreword by Justin Kaplan

Little, Brown and Company
NEW YORK   BOSTON

Copyright © 2005 by Little, Brown and Company
Foreword copyright © 2005 by Justin Kaplan

All rights reserved. No part of this book may be reproduced in any form
or by any electronic or mechanical means, including information storage
and retrieval systems, without permission in writing from the publisher,
except by a reviewer who may quote brief passages in a review.

Little, Brown and Company
Time Warner Book Group
1271 Avenue of the Americas, New York, NY 10020
Visit our Web site at www.twbookmark.com

First Edition: October 2005

The quotations in this book are from *Bartlett's Familiar Quotations*,
Seventeenth Edition, Justin Kaplan, General Editor.

Library of Congress Cataloging-in-Publication Data

Shakespeare, William, 1564–1616.
    Bartlett's Shakespeare quotations / [compiled by] John Bartlett;
  Foreword by Justin Kaplan—1st ed.
        p.   cm.
    Selected quotes from: Bartlett's familiar quotations / John Bartlett.
  17th ed. 2002.
    ISBN 0-316-01419-2
    1. Shakespeare, William, 1564–1616 — Quotations.   I. Title:
  Shakespeare quotations.   II. Bartlett, John, 1820–1905.   III. Kaplan,
  Justin.   IV. Bartlett, John, 1820–1905. Bartlett's familiar quotations.
  V. Title.

PR2892.B33 2005
822.3'3 — dc22   2005050432

10   9   8   7   6   5   4   3   2   1

Q-FF

Printed in the United States of America

Contents

Foreword by Justin Kaplan   vii

King Henry the Sixth, Part I   3
King Henry the Sixth, Part II   4
King Henry the Sixth, Part III   7
Venus and Adonis   10
King Richard the Third   11
The Comedy of Errors   16
The Rape of Lucrece   17
Titus Andronicus   19
The Taming of the Shrew   19
The Two Gentlemen of Verona   22
Love's Labour's Lost   23
King John   29
King Richard the Second   34
A Midsummer-Night's Dream   42
Romeo and Juliet   50

King Henry the Fourth, Part 1	59
The Merchant of Venice	71
The Merry Wives of Windsor	85
King Henry the Fourth, Part II	88
King Henry the Fifth	94
Much Ado About Nothing	101
Julius Caesar	107
As You Like It	118
Hamlet	130
The Phoenix and the Turtle	162
Troilus and Cressida	162
Twelfth-Night	169
All's Well That Ends Well	177
Measure for Measure	179
Othello	185
King Lear	200
Timon of Athens	214
Macbeth	215
Antony and Cleopatra	235
Coriolanus	244
Pericles	246
Cymbeline	247
Sonnets	249
The Winter's Tale	260
The Tempest	264
King Henry the Eighth	270
Shakespeare's Epitaph	275

Foreword

In 1855, John Bartlett, a Cambridge, Massachusetts, bookseller and self-educated scholar, first published the volume of quotations that today, greatly expanded and brought up-to-date to reflect modern taste, needs, and usage, still bears his name. By the time of his death in 1905 at the age of eighty-five, he had made his name as generic for quotations as Noah Webster's is for dictionary definitions. His declared aim was to show "the obligations our language owes to various authors for numerous phrases and familiar quotations which have become 'household words.'" (You'll find the phrase "household words" in Shakespeare's *Henry V.*)

The prime components of Bartlett's original edition were the King James Bible and the works of Shakespeare. By a remarkable, even miraculous, confluence of cultural forces, these two wellsprings of literature and English language as we now know it came into being within a decade or so of each other. By 1604, the year King James I convened a conference of scholars and translators at Hampton Court and commissioned them to prepare an "Authorized Version" of the Bible, more than a dozen of Shakespeare's plays, including *Hamlet*, were already in print. The translators finished their work in 1611, a year that also saw a performance of Shakespeare's *The Tempest* at the royal court.

This collection of about two thousand familiar and essential passages from Shakespeare is drawn from the seventeenth edition of *Bartlett's Familiar Quotations* (2002). Contemporary appreciation of Shakespeare differs somewhat from that of John Bartlett and his near successors, who tended to value the tragedies at the expense of the comedies and poems. Recent editors have tried to correct the balance. In any case, you'll find more Shakespeare in the current edition of *Bartlett's* than ever before: eloquent and memorable passages of a sort that Matthew Arnold called "touchstones" because they meet the tests and also set the standards of highest excellence. In obedience to modern taste and usage, the space *Bartlett's* gives to some other major English writers, Alexander Pope, for example, has been abridged rather than expanded over the years. But Shakespeare, as his contemporary Ben Jonson recognized, "was not of an age, but for all time!" At the very least this collection can serve as an informal concordance to Shakespeare, a quiz and game book, and a memory jogger that invites you to sample and then go deeper into one of the glories of world literature. "Brush up your Shakespeare," says Cole Porter's lyric in *Kiss Me, Kate.* "Start quoting him now."

"Mr. William Shakespeare was born at Stratford upon Avon in the County of Warwick," the biographer and antiquarian John Aubrey wrote in 1690. "His father was a butcher, and I have been told heretofore by some of the neighbors that when he was a boy he exercised his father's trade, but when he killed a calf he would do it in a high style and make a speech." According to other accounts, in his early years he may have been a country schoolteacher, a member of a company of traveling players, and a fugitive from justice for poaching deer. Despite his shadowy and unpromising past, the work of this small-town Englishman, the beneficiary of only a provincial grammar school education, has been translated, performed, and read in virtually every human tongue.

How Shakespeare managed to know so much and understand it so incomparably no one can explain. Never doubted in his lifetime or for several centuries after, starting in the mid-nineteenth century, Shakespeare's authorship of the plays and poems attributed to him began to be questioned. Among the candidates put forward to replace him as sole and true author of the tragedies, comedies, history plays, and poems have been Francis Bacon (his identity supposedly hidden in codes and ciphers), the Earl of Oxford, and others endowed with high birth and a university education. According to the anti-Stratfordian argument, someone with Shakespeare's rudimentary education, obscure position in society, and apparent lack of legal and classical learning and of personal familiarity with the tangled affairs of kings and queens should not have been capable of writing what and as he did. The same narrow logic, although espoused by Sigmund Freud, among others, discounts the role of genius in the work of "our *myriad-minded* Shakespeare," as Coleridge called him. Shakespeare's authorship of the works of Shakespeare remains secure, the controversy easily defused by the joke that if William Shakespeare did not write his works, someone else with the same name did.

"Of all modern, and perhaps ancient poets," John Dryden wrote in 1666, Shakespeare "had the largest and most comprehensive soul." "He was not a man, he was a continent," Gustave Flaubert wrote. "He contained whole crowds of great men, entire landscapes." "Shakespeare is the Canon," the critic Harold Bloom writes. "He sets the standards and the limits of literature." Quotable quotations about Shakespeare are a category in themselves.

Bartlett's Shakespeare is also a reminder of the extent to which the work of this greatest of English-language poets and dramatists has entered and formed our daily speech without our necessarily being aware of it. We say "sink or swim" but probably don't realize that we may be quoting from *Henry IV, Part I*. Comparably, many other Shakespearean phrases, idioms, and images have worked their way into daily discourse: "Forever and a day" (*As You Like It*), for example, and "So much for him" (*Hamlet*), "In my mind's eye" (*Hamlet* again), "Play the villain" (*Othello*), "We have seen better days" (*Timon of Athens*), "A charmed life" and "Out, damned spot!" (*Macbeth*), "More sinn'd against than sinning" and "Every inch a king" (*King Lear*), "What's in a name?" and "Star-cross'd lovers" (*Romeo and Juliet*), "My salad days" (*Antony and Cleopatra*), "We happy few" (*Henry V*), and, almost inevitably, "Let's kill all the lawyers" (*Henry VI, Part II*). Such phrases are part of the language that most literate people use, a telegraphic or shorthand common tongue composed of quotations and allusions that surface from an almost pre-intellectual level of consciousness. We use these fragments to add point and luster to our own utterances.

For about five centuries the plays and poems of Shakespeare have formed the air we breathe and the blood in our veins. It's possible that even the semiliterate Mississippi Valley "lunkheads" Mark Twain portrayed in *Huckleberry Finn* enjoyed a greater intimacy with at least a few of the tragedies and history plays of Shakespeare than many educated people do today. According to a venerable anecdote, someone seeing *Hamlet* for the first time is supposed to have complained, on leaving the theater, that he couldn't understand what all the fuss was about. "*Hamlet* sounds like just a lot of familiar quotations strung together."

Justin Kaplan

BARTLETT'S SHAKESPEARE QUOTATIONS

KING HENRY THE SIXTH, PART I [1589–1590]

Hung be the heavens with black, yield day
to night! *Act I, sc. i, l. 1*

Fight till the last gasp. *I, ii, 127*

Expect Saint Martin's summer, halcyon days. *I, ii, 131*

Glory is like a circle in the water,
Which never ceaseth to enlarge itself,
Till by broad spreading it disperse to nought. *I, ii, 133*

Unbidden guests
Are often welcomest when they are gone. *II, ii, 55*

Between two hawks, which flies the higher pitch;
Between two dogs, which hath the deeper mouth;
Between two blades, which bears the better temper;
Between two horses, which doth bear him best;
Between two girls, which hath the merriest eye;
I have perhaps, some shallow spirit of judgment;
But in these nice sharp quillets of the law,
Good faith, I am no wiser than a daw. *II, iv, 12*

I'll note you in my book of memory. *II, iv, 101*

Just death, kind umpire of men's miseries. *II, v, 29*

Chok'd with ambition of the meaner sort. *II, v, 123*

Delays have dangerous ends. *III, ii, 33*

Of all base passions, fear is most accurs'd. *V, ii, 18*

She's beautiful and therefore to be woo'd,
She is a woman, therefore to be won. *V, iii, 78*

For what is wedlock forced, but a hell,
An age of discord and continual strife?
Whereas the contrary bringeth bliss,
And is a pattern of celestial peace. *V, v, 62*

KING HENRY THE SIXTH, PART II [*1590–1591*]

'Tis not my speeches that you do mislike,
But 'tis my presence that doth trouble ye.
Rancor will out. *Act I, sc. i, l. 141*

Could I come near your beauty with my nails
I'd set my ten commandments in your face. *I, iii, 144*

Forbear to judge, for we are sinners all.
Close up his eyes, and draw the curtain close;
And let us all to meditation. *III, iii, 31*

The gaudy, blabbing, and remorseful day
Is crept into the bosom of the sea. *IV, i, 1*

Small things make base men proud. *IV, i, 106*

True nobility is exempt from fear. *IV, i, 129*

I will make it felony to drink small beer. *IV, ii, 75*

The first thing we do, let's kill all the lawyers. *IV, ii, 86*

Is not this a lamentable thing, that of the skin of an
innocent lamb should be made parchment? that
parchment, being scribbled o'er, should undo a man?
IV, ii, 88

Adam was a gardener. *IV, ii, 146*

Blessed are the peacemakers on earth. *II, i, 34*

Now, God be prais'd, that to believing souls
Gives light in darkness, comfort in despair! *II, i, 66*

God defend the right! *II, iii, 55*

Sometimes hath the brightest day a cloud;
And after summer evermore succeeds
Barren winter, with his wrathful nipping cold:
So cares and joys abound, as seasons fleet. *II, iv, 1*

Now 'tis the spring, and weeds are shallow-rooted;
Suffer them now and they'll o'ergrow the garden. *III, i, 31*

In thy face I see
The map of honor, truth, and loyalty. *III, i, 202*

What stronger breastplate than a heart untainted!
Thrice is he arm'd that hath his quarrel just,
And he but naked, though lock'd up in steel,
Whose conscience with injustice is corrupted. *III, ii, 232*

He dies, and makes no sign. *III, iii, 29*

Thou hast most traitorously corrupted the youth of
the realm in erecting a grammar-school; and whereas,
before, our forefathers had no other books but the
score and the tally, thou hast caused printing to be
used; and, contrary to the king, his crown, and
dignity, thou hast built a paper-mill. *IV, vii,* 35

KING HENRY THE SIXTH, PART III [1590–1591]

Beggars mounted run their horse to death. *Act I, sc. iv, l.* 127

O tiger's heart wrapp'd in a woman's hide! *I, iv,* 137

To weep is to make less the depth of grief. *II, i,* 85

The smallest worm will turn being trodden on. *II, ii,* 17

Didst thou never hear
That things ill got had ever bad success? *II, ii,* 45

Thou [Death] setter up and plucker down of kings.
II, iii, 37

And what makes robbers bold but too much lenity?
II, vi, 22

My crown is in my heart, not on my head;
Not deck'd with diamonds and Indian stones,
Nor to be seen: my crown is call'd content;
A crown it is that seldom kings enjoy. *III, i, 62*

'Tis a happy thing
To be the father unto many sons. *III, ii, 104*

Like one that stands upon a promontory,
And spies a far-off shore where he would tread,
Wishing his foot were equal with his eye. *III, ii, 135*

Yield not thy neck
To fortune's yoke, but let thy dauntless mind
Still ride in triumph over all mischance. *III, iii, 16*

For how can tyrants safely govern home,
Unless abroad they purchase great alliance? *III, iii, 69*

Having nothing, nothing can he lose. *III, iii, 152*

Hasty marriage seldom proveth well. *IV, i, 18*

What fates impose, that men must needs abide;
It boots not to resist both wind and tide. *IV, iii, 57*

Now join your hands, and with your hands your
hearts. *IV, vi, 39*

For many men that stumble at the threshold
Are well foretold that danger lurks within. *IV, vii, 11*

A little fire is quickly trodden out,
Which, being suffer'd, rivers cannot quench. *IV, viii, 7*

When the lion fawns upon the lamb,
The lamb will never cease to follow him. *IV, viii, 49*

What is pomp, rule, reign, but earth and dust?
And, live we how we can, yet die we must. *V, ii, 27*

For every cloud engenders not a storm. *V, iii, 13*

What though the mast be now blown overboard,
The cable broke, the holding anchor lost,
And half our sailors swallow'd in the flood?
Yet lives our pilot still. *V, iv, 3*

So part we sadly in this troublous world,
To meet with joy in sweet Jerusalem. *V, v, 7*

Men ne'er spend their fury on a child. *V, v, 57*

He's sudden if a thing comes in his head. *V, v, 86*

Suspicion always haunts the guilty mind;
The thief doth fear each bush an officer. *V, vi, 11*

This word "love," which greybeards call divine. *V, vi, 81*

VENUS AND ADONIS [1592]

Bid me discourse, I will enchant thine ear. *l. 145*

Love is a spirit all compact of fire,
Not gross to sink, but light, and will aspire. *l. 149*

"Fondling," she saith, "since I have hemm'd thee here
Within the circuit of this ivory pale,
I'll be a park, and thou shalt be my deer;
Feed where thou wilt, on mountain, or in dale:
Graze on my lips, and if those hills be dry,
Stray lower, where the pleasant fountains lie." *l. 229*

O! what a war of looks was then between them. *l. 355*

Like a red morn, that ever yet betoken'd
Wrack to the seaman, tempest to the field. *l. 453*

The owl, night's herald. *l. 531*

Love comforteth like sunshine after rain. *l. 799*

The text is old, the orator too green. *l. 806*

For he being dead, with him is beauty slain,
And, beauty dead, black chaos comes again. *l. 1019*

The grass stoops not, she treads on it so light. *l. 1028*

KING RICHARD THE THIRD [1592–1593]

Now is the winter of our discontent
Made glorious summer by this sun of York. *Act I, sc. i, l. 1*

Grim-visag'd war hath smooth'd his wrinkled front.

I, i, 9

He capers nimbly in a lady's chamber
To the lascivious pleasing of a lute. *I, i, 12*

This weak piping time of peace. *I, i, 24*

No beast so fierce but knows some touch of pity.
I, ii, 71

Look, how my ring encompasseth thy finger,
Even so thy breast encloseth my poor heart;
Wear both of them, for both of them are thine. *I, ii, 204*

Was ever woman in this humor woo'd?
Was ever woman in this humor won? *I, ii, 229*

The world is grown so bad
That wrens make prey where eagles dare not perch.
I, iii, 70

The day will come that thou shalt wish for me
To help thee curse this pois'nous bunch-back'd toad.
I, iii, 245

And thus I clothe my naked villany
With odd old ends stol'n forth of holy writ,
And seem a saint when most I play the devil. *I, iii, 336*

Talkers are no good doers. *I, iii, 351*

O, I have pass'd a miserable night,
So full of ugly sights, of ghastly dreams,
That, as I am a Christian faithful man,
I would not spend another such a night,
Though 'twere to buy a world of happy days. *I, iv, 2*

Lord, Lord! methought what pain it was to drown:
What dreadful noise of water in mine ears!
What sights of ugly death within mine eyes!
Methought I saw a thousand fearful wracks;
A thousand men that fishes gnaw'd upon. *I, iv, 21*

The kingdom of perpetual night. *I, iv, 47*

Sorrow breaks seasons and reposing hours,
Makes the night morning, and the noontide night.
I, iv, 76

A parlous boy. *II, iv, 35*

So wise so young, they say, do never live long. *III, i, 79*

Off with his head! *III, iv, 75*

Lives like a drunken sailor on a mast;
Ready with every nod to tumble down
Into the fatal bowels of the deep. *III, iv, 98*

I am not in the giving vein today. *IV, ii, 115*

The sons of Edward sleep in Abraham's bosom.
IV, iii, 38

A grievous burden was thy birth to me;
Tetchy and wayward was thy infancy. *IV, iv, 168*

An honest tale speeds best being plainly told. *IV, iv, 359*

Harp not on that string. *IV, iv, 365*

Relenting fool, and shallow changing woman! *IV, iv, 432*

Is the chair empty? is the sword unsway'd?
Is the king dead? the empire unpossess'd? *IV, iv, 470*

True hope is swift, and flies with swallow's wings;
Kings it makes gods, and meaner creatures kings.
V, ii, 23

The king's name is a tower of strength. *V, iii, 12*

Give me another horse! bind up my wounds! *V, iii, 178*

O coward conscience, how dost thou afflict me!
V, iii, 180

My conscience hath a thousand several tongues,
And every tongue brings in a several tale,
And every tale condemns me for a villain. *V, iii, 194*

Conscience is but a word that cowards use,
Devis'd at first to keep the strong in awe. *V, iii, 310*

A horse! a horse! my kingdom for a horse! *V, iv, 7*

I have set my life upon a cast,
And I will stand the hazard of the die.
I think there be six Richmonds in the field. *V, iv, 9*

THE COMEDY OF ERRORS [1592–1594]

The pleasing punishment that women bear. *Act I, sc. i, l. 46*

For we may pity, though not pardon thee. *I, i, 97*

Why, headstrong liberty is lash'd with woe.
There's nothing situate under heaven's eye
But hath his bound, in earth, in sea, in sky. *II, i, 15*

Every why hath a wherefore. *II, ii, 45*

There's no time for a man to recover his hair that
grows bald by nature. *II, ii, 74*

What he hath scanted men in hair, he hath given
them in wit. *II, ii, 83*

Small cheer and great welcome makes a merry feast.
III, i, 26

There is something in the wind. *III, i, 69*

We'll pluck a crow together. *III, i, 83*

For slander lives upon succession,
Forever housed where it gets possession. *III, i,* 105

Be not thy tongue thy own shame's orator. *III, ii,* 10

Ill deeds are doubled with an evil word. *III, ii,* 20

A back-friend, a shoulder-clapper. *IV, ii,* 37

The venom clamors of a jealous woman
Poison more deadly than a mad dog's tooth. *V, i,* 69

Unquiet meals make ill digestions. *V, i,* 74

One Pinch, a hungry lean-fac'd villain,
A mere anatomy, a mountebank,
A threadbare juggler, and a fortune-teller,
A needy, hollow-ey'd, sharp-looking wretch,
A living-dead man. *V, i,* 238

THE RAPE OF LUCRECE *[1593–1594]*

Beauty itself doth of itself persuade
The eyes of men without an orator. *l.* 29

This silent war of lilies and of roses,
Which Tarquin view'd in her fair face's field. *l. 71*

One for all, or all for one we gage. *l. 144*

Who buys a minute's mirth to wail a week?
Or sells eternity to get a toy?
For one sweet grape who will the vine destroy? *l. 213*

Extreme fear can neither fight nor fly. *l. 230*

All orators are dumb when beauty pleadeth. *l. 268*

Time's glory is to calm contending kings,
To unmask falsehood and bring truth to light. *l. 939*

For greatest scandal waits on greatest state. *l. 1006*

To see sad sights moves more than hear them told.
l. 1324

Cloud-kissing Ilion. *l. 1370*

Lucrece swears he did her wrong. *l. 1462*

TITUS ANDRONICUS [*1593–1594*]

Sweet mercy is nobility's true badge. *Act I, sc. i, l. 1*

These words are razors to my wounded heart. *I, i, 314*

He lives in fame that died in virtue's cause. *I, i, 390*

These dreary dumps. *I, i, 391*

The eagle suffers little birds to sing,
And is not careful what they mean thereby. *IV, iv, 82*

Tut! I have done a thousand dreadful things
As willingly as one would kill a fly. *V, i, 141*

THE TAMING OF THE SHREW [*1593–1594*]

I'll not budge an inch. *Induction, sc. i, l. 13*

And if the boy have not a woman's gift
To rain a shower of commanded tears,
An onion will do well for such a shift. *i, 124*

No profit grows where is no pleasure ta'en;
In brief, sir, study what you most affect. *Act I, sc. i, l. 39*

There's small choice in rotten apples. *I, i, 137*

To seek their fortunes further than at home,
Where small experience grows. *I, ii, 51*

I come to wive it wealthily in Padua. *I, ii, 75*

Nothing comes amiss, so money comes withal. *I, ii, 82*

And do as adversaries do in law,
Strive mightily, but eat and drink as friends. *I, ii, 281*

I must dance barefoot on her wedding day,
And, for your love to her, lead apes in hell. *II, i, 33*

Asses are made to bear, and so are you. *II, i, 200*

Kiss me, Kate, we will be married o' Sunday. *II, i, 318*

Old fashions please me best. *III, i, 81*

Who woo'd in haste and means to wed at leisure. *III, ii, 11*

Such an injury would vex a very saint. *III, ii,* 28

A little pot and soon hot. *IV, i,* 6

Sits as one new-risen from a dream. *IV, i,* 189

This is a way to kill a wife with kindness. *IV, i,* 211

Kindness in women, not their beauteous looks,
Shall win my love. *IV, ii,* 41

Our purses shall be proud, our garments poor:
For 'tis the mind that makes the body rich;
And as the sun breaks through the darkest clouds,
So honor peereth in the meanest habit. *IV, iii,* 173

Forward, I pray, since we have come so far,
And be it moon, or sun, or what you please.
An if you please to call it a rush-candle,
Henceforth I vow it shall be so for me. *IV, v,* 12

He that is giddy thinks the world turns round. *V, ii,* 20

A woman mov'd is like a fountain troubled,
Muddy, ill-seeming, thick, bereft of beauty. *V, ii,* 143

Such duty as the subject owes the prince,
Even such a woman oweth to her husband. *V, ii, 156*

THE TWO GENTLEMEN OF VERONA [1594]

Home-keeping youth have ever homely wits. *Act I, sc. i, l. 2*

I have no other but a woman's reason:
I think him so, because I think him so. *I, ii, 23*

Julia: They do not love that do not show their love.
Lucetta: O! they love least that let men know their love.
I, ii, 31

O! how this spring of love resembleth
The uncertain glory of an April day! *I, iii, 84*

O jest unseen, inscrutable, invisible,
As a nose on a man's face, or a weathercock on a
steeple! *II, i, 145*

He makes sweet music with th' enamell'd stones. *II, vii, 28*

That man that hath a tongue, I say, is no man,
If with his tongue he cannot win a woman. *III, i, 104*

Except I be by Silvia in the night,
There is no music in the nightingale. *III, i, 178*

Much is the force of heaven-bred poesy. *III, ii, 72*

Who is Silvia? what is she,
That all our swains commend her?
Holy, fair, and wise is she;
The heaven such grace did lend her,
That she might admired be. *IV, ii, 40*

Alas, how love can trifle with itself! *IV, iv, 190*

Black men are pearls in beauteous ladies' eyes. *V, ii, 12*

How use doth breed a habit in a man! *V, iv, 1*

LOVE'S LABOUR'S LOST [1594–1595]

Spite of cormorant devouring Time. *Act I, sc. i, l. 4*

Make us heirs of all eternity. *I, i, 7*

Why, all delights are vain; but that most vain
Which, with pain purchas'd doth inherit pain. *I, i, 72*

Light seeking light doth light of light beguile. *I, i, 77*

Study is like the heaven's glorious sun,
That will not be deep-search'd with saucy looks;
Small have continual plodders ever won,
Save base authority from others' books.
These earthly godfathers of heaven's lights
That give a name to every fixed star,
Have no more profit of their shining nights
Than those that walk and wot not what they are.
I, i, 84

At Christmas I no more desire a rose
Than wish a snow in May's newfangled mirth;
But like of each thing that in season grows. *I, i, 105*

And men sit down to that nourishment which is called
supper. *I, i, 237*

That unlettered small-knowing soul. *I, i, 251*

A child of our grandmother Eve, a female; or, for thy
more sweet understanding, a woman. *I, i, 263*

Affliction may one day smile again; and till then, sit
thee down, sorrow! *I, i, 312*

Devise, wit; write, pen; for I am for whole volumes in
folio.   *I, ii, 194*

Beauty is bought by judgment of the eye,
Not utter'd by base sale of chapmen's tongues.   *II, i, 15*

A merrier man,
Within the limit of becoming mirth,
I never spent an hour's talk withal.   *II, i, 66*

Your wit's too hot, it speeds too fast, 'twill tire.   *II, i, 119*

Warble, child; make passionate my sense of hearing.
III, i, 1

Remuneration! O! that's the Latin word for three
farthings.   *III, i, 143*

A very beadle to a humorous sigh.   *III, i, 185*

This wimpled, whining, purblind, wayward boy,
This senior-junior, giant-dwarf, Dan Cupid;
Regent of love-rimes, lord of folded arms,
The anointed sovereign of sighs and groans,
Liege of all loiters and malcontents.   *III, i, 189*

He hath not fed of the dainties that are bred of a book; he hath not eat paper, as it were; he hath not drunk ink. *IV, ii, 25*

Many can brook the weather that love not the wind.
IV, ii, 34

You two are book-men. *IV, ii, 35*

These are begot in the ventricle of memory, nourished in the womb of pia mater, and delivered upon the mellowing of occasion. *IV, ii, 70*

By heaven, I do love, and it hath taught me to rime, and to be melancholy. *IV, iii, 13*

The heavenly rhetoric of thine eye. *IV, iii, 60*

For where is any author in the world
Teaches such beauty as a woman's eye?
Learning is but an adjunct to ourself. *IV, iii, 312*

But love, first learned in a lady's eyes,
Lives not alone immured in the brain. *IV, iii, 327*

It adds a precious seeing to the eye. *IV, iii, 333*

As sweet and musical
As bright Apollo's lute, strung with his hair;
And when Love speaks, the voice of all the gods
Makes heaven drowsy with the harmony. *IV, iii, 342*

From women's eyes this doctrine I derive:
They sparkle still the right Promethean fire;
They are the books, the arts, the academes,
That show, contain, and nourish all the world.
IV, iii, 350

He draweth out the thread of his verbosity finer than
the staple of his argument. *V, i, 18*

Moth: They have been at a great feast of languages,
and stolen the scraps.
Costard: O! they have lived long on the almsbasket of
words. I marvel thy master hath not eaten thee for a
word; for thou art not so long by the head as
honorificabilitudinitatibus: thou art easier swallowed than
a flap-dragon. *V, i, 39*

In the posteriors of this day, which the rude multitude
call the afternoon. *V, i, 96*

Taffeta phrases, silken terms precise,
Three-pil'd hyperboles, spruce affectation,
Figures pedantical. *V, ii,* 407

Let me take you a button-hole lower. *V, ii,* 705

The naked truth of it is, I have no shirt. *V, ii,* 715

A jest's prosperity lies in the ear
Of him that hears it, never in the tongue
Of him that makes it. *V, ii,* 869

When daisies pied and violets blue,
And lady-smocks all silver-white,
And cuckoo-buds of yellow hue
Do paint the meadows with delight,
The cuckoo then, on every tree,
Mocks married men; for thus sings he,
Cuckoo;
Cuckoo, cuckoo: O word of fear,
Unpleasing to a married ear! *V, ii,* 902

When icicles hang by the wall,
And Dick the shepherd blows his nail,
And Tom bears logs into the hall,
And milk comes frozen home in pail,

When blood is nipp'd and ways be foul,
Then nightly sings the staring owl,
    Tu-who;
Tu-whit, tu-who — a merry note,
While greasy Joan doth keel the pot. *V, ii,* 920

When all aloud the wind doth blow,
And coughing drowns the parson's saw,
And birds sit brooding in the snow,
And Marian's nose looks red and raw,
When roasted crabs hiss in the bowl. *V, ii,* 929

The words of Mercury are harsh after the songs of
Apollo. *V, ii,* 938

KING JOHN [1594–1596]

For new-made honor doth forget men's names.
Act I, sc. i, l. 187

Sweet, sweet, sweet poison for the age's tooth.
I, i, 213

Bearing their birthrights proudly on their backs,
To make a hazard of new fortunes here. *II, i,* 70

For courage mounteth with occasion. *II, i, 82*

The hare of whom the proverb goes,
Whose valor plucks dead lions by the beard. *II, i, 137*

A woman's will. *II, i, 194*

Saint George, that swing'd the dragon, and e'er since
Sits on his horse back at mine hostess' door. *II, i, 288*

He is the half part of a blessed man,
Left to be finished by such a she;
And she a fair divided excellence,
Whose fullness of perfection lies in him. *II, i, 437*

'Zounds! I was never so bethump'd with words
Since I first call'd my brother's father dad. *II, i, 466*

Mad world! mad kings, mad composition! *II, i, 561*

That smooth-fac'd gentleman, tickling Commodity,
Commodity, the bias of the world. *II, i, 573*

I will instruct my sorrows to be proud;
For grief is proud and makes his owner stoop. *III, i, 68*

Thou wear a lion's hide! doff it for shame,
And hang a calf's-skin on those recreant limbs.
III, i, 128

The sun's o'ercast with blood: fair day, adieu!
Which is the side that I must go withal?
I am with both: each army hath a hand;
And in their rage, I having hold of both,
They whirl asunder and dismember me. *III, i, 326*

Bell, book, and candle shall not drive me back.
III, iii, 12

Look, who comes here! a grave unto a soul. *III, iv, 17*

Death, death: O, amiable lovely death! *III, iv, 25*

Grief fills the room up of my absent child,
Lies in his bed, walks up and down with me,
Puts on his pretty looks, repeats his words,
Remembers me of all his gracious parts,
Stuffs out his vacant garments with his form.
III, iv, 93

Life is as tedious as a twice-told tale,
Vexing the dull ear of a drowsy man. *III, iv, 108*

When Fortune means to men most good,
She looks upon them with a threatening eye. *III, iv,* 119

A scepter snatch'd with an unruly hand
Must be as boisterously maintain'd as gain'd;
And he that stands upon a slippery place
Makes nice of no vile hold to stay him up. *III, iv,* 135

As quiet as a lamb. *IV, i,* 80

To gild refined gold, to paint the lily,
To throw a perfume on the violet,
To smooth the ice, or add another hue
Unto the rainbow, or with taper-light
To seek the beauteous eye of heaven to garnish,
Is wasteful and ridiculous excess. *IV, ii,* 11

And oftentimes excusing of a fault
Doth make the fault the worse by the excuse. *IV, ii,* 30

We cannot hold mortality's strong hand. *IV, ii,* 82

There is no sure foundation set on blood,
No certain life achiev'd by others' death. *IV, ii,* 104

Make haste; the better foot before. *IV, ii, 170*

Another lean unwash'd artificer. *IV, ii, 201*

How oft the sight of means to do ill deeds
Makes ill deeds done! *IV, ii, 219*

Heaven take my soul, and England keep my bones!
IV, iii, 10

I am amaz'd, methinks, and lose my way
Among the thorns and dangers of this world. *IV, iii, 140*

Unthread the rude eye of rebellion,
And welcome home again discarded faith. *V, iv, 11*

The day shall not be up so soon as I,
To try the fair adventure of tomorrow. *V, v, 21*

'Tis strange that death should sing.
I am the cygnet to this pale faint swan,
Who chants a doleful hymn to his own death. *V, vii, 20*

Now my soul hath elbow-room. *V, vii, 28*

I do not ask you much:
I beg cold comfort. *V, vii, 41*

This England never did, nor never shall,
Lie at the proud foot of a conqueror. *V, vii, 112*

Come the three corners of the world in arms,
And we shall shock them. Nought shall make us rue,
If England to itself do rest but true. *V, vii, 116*

KING RICHARD THE SECOND [1595]

The purest treasure mortal times afford
Is spotless reputation. *Act I, sc. i, l. 177*

Mine honor is my life; both grow in one;
Take honor from me, and my life is done. *I, i, 182*

We were not born to sue, but to command. *I, i, 196*

The daintiest last, to make the end most sweet. *I, iii, 68*

Truth hath a quiet breast. *I, iii, 96*

How long a time lies in one little word! *I, iii, 213*

Things sweet to taste prove in digestion sour.
                    I, iii, 236

Must I not serve a long apprenticehood
    To foreign passages, and in the end,
Having my freedom, boast of nothing else
But that I was a journeyman to grief? *I, iii, 271*

All places that the eye of heaven visits
Are to a wise man ports and happy havens.
    Teach thy necessity to reason thus;
        There is no virtue like necessity.
    Think not the king did banish thee,
        But thou the king. *I, iii, 275*

For gnarling sorrow hath less power to bite
The man that mocks at it and sets it light.
                    I, iii, 292

O! who can hold a fire in his hand
By thinking on the frosty Caucasus?
Or cloy the hungry edge of appetite
    By bare imagination of a feast?
Or wallow naked in December snow

By thinking on fantastic summer's heat?
O, no! the apprehension of the good
Gives but the greater feeling to the worse. *I, iii, 294*

Where'er I wander, boast of this I can,
Though banish'd, yet a true-born Englishman. *I, iii, 308*

The tongues of dying men
Enforce attention like deep harmony. *II, i, 5*

The setting sun, and music at the close,
As the last taste of sweets, is sweetest last,
Writ in remembrance more than things long past.

II, i, 12

Report of fashions in proud Italy,
Whose manners still our tardy apish nation
Limps after in base imitation. *II, i, 21*

For violent fires soon burn out themselves;
Small showers last long, but sudden storms are short.

II, i, 34

This royal throne of kings, this scepter'd isle,
This earth of majesty, this seat of Mars,
This other Eden, demi-paradise,
This fortress built by Nature for herself
Against infection and the hand of war,
This happy breed of men, this little world,
This precious stone set in the silver sea,
Which serves it in the office of a wall,
Or as a moat defensive to a house,
Against the envy of less happier lands,
This blessed plot, this earth, this realm, this England,
This nurse, this teeming womb of royal kings,
Fear'd by their breed and famous by their birth. *II, i,* 40

England, bound in with the triumphant sea,
Whose rocky shore beats back the envious siege
Of watery Neptune. *II, i,* 61

That England, that was wont to conquer others,
Hath made a shameful conquest of itself. *II, i,* 65

The ripest fruit first falls. *II, i,* 154

Each substance of a grief hath twenty shadows. *II, ii,* 14

I count myself in nothing else so happy
As in a soul remembering my good friends.

II, iii, 46

Evermore thanks, the exchequer of the poor. *II, iii, 65*

Grace me no grace, nor uncle me no uncle. *II, iii, 87*

The caterpillars of the commonwealth,
Which I have sworn to weed and pluck away.

II, iii, 166

Things past redress are now with me past care.

II, iii, 171

I see thy glory like a shooting star
Fall to the base earth from the firmament.

II, iv, 19

Eating the bitter bread of banishment. *III, i, 21*

Not all the water in the rough rude sea
Can wash the balm from an anointed king.

III, ii, 54

O! call back yesterday, bid time return. *III, ii, 69*

The worst is death, and death will have his day.
III, ii, 103

Of comfort no man speak:
Let's talk of graves, of worms, and epitaphs;
Make dust our paper, and with rainy eyes
Write sorrow on the bosom of the earth;
Let's choose executors and talk of wills. *III, ii, 144*

And nothing can we call our own but death,
And that small model of the barren earth
Which serves as paste and cover to our bones.
For God's sake, let us sit upon the ground
And tell sad stories of the death of kings:
How some have been depos'd, some slain in war,
Some haunted by the ghosts they have depos'd,
Some poison'd by their wives, some sleeping kill'd,
All murder'd: for within the hollow crown
That rounds the mortal temples of a king
Keeps Death his court. *III, ii, 152*

Comes at the last, and with a little pin
Bores through his castle wall, and farewell king!
III, ii, 169

He is come to open
The purple testament of bleeding war. *III, iii, 93*

O! that I were as great
As is my grief, or lesser than my name,
Or that I could forget what I have been,
Or not remember what I must be now. *III, iii, 136*

I'll give my jewels for a set of beads,
My gorgeous palace for a hermitage,
My gay apparel for an almsman's gown.
III, iii, 147

And my large kingdom for a little grave,
A little little grave, an obscure grave. *III, iii, 153*

And there at Venice gave
His body to that pleasant country's earth,
And his pure soul unto his captain Christ,
Under whose colors he had fought so long. *IV, i, 97*

Peace shall go sleep with Turks and infidels.
IV, i, 139

So Judas did to Christ: but he, in twelve,
Found truth in all but one; I, in twelve thousand, none.
God save the king! Will no man say, amen? *IV, i,* 170

Now is this golden crown like a deep well
That owes two buckets filling one another;
The emptier ever dancing in the air,
The other down, unseen and full of water:
That bucket down and full of tears am I,
Drinking my griefs, whilst you mount up on high.
IV, i, 184

You may my glories and my state depose,
But not my griefs; still am I king of those. *IV, i,* 192

Some of you with Pilate wash your hands,
Showing an outward pity. *IV, i,* 239

A mockery king of snow. *IV, i,* 260

As in a theater, the eyes of men,
After a well-grac'd actor leaves the stage,
Are idly bent on him that enters next,
Thinking his prattle to be tedious. *V, ii,* 23

How sour sweet music is
When time is broke and no proportion kept!
So is it in the music of men's lives. *V, v, 42*

I wasted time, and now doth time waste me;
For now hath time made me his numbering clock:
My thoughts are minutes. *V, v, 49*

This music mads me: let it sound no more. *V, v, 61*

Mount, mount, my soul! thy seat is up on high,
Whilst my gross flesh sinks downward, here to die.
V, v, 112

A MIDSUMMER-NIGHT'S DREAM [1595–1596]

To live a barren sister all your life,
Chanting faint hymns to the cold fruitless moon.
Act I, sc. i, l. 72

For aught that I could ever read,
Could ever hear by tale or history,
The course of true love never did run smooth. *I, i, 132*

Swift as a shadow, short as any dream,
Brief as the lightning in the collied night,
That, in a spleen, unfolds both heaven and earth,
And ere a man hath power to say, "Behold!"
The jaws of darkness do devour it up:
So quick bright things come to confusion. *I, i, 144*

Love looks not with the eyes, but with the mind,
And therefore is wing'd Cupid painted blind. *I, i, 234*

The most lamentable comedy, and most cruel death of
Pyramus and Thisby. *I, ii, 11*

Masters, spread yourselves. *I, ii, 16*

This is Ercles' vein, a tyrant's vein. *I, ii, 43*

I'll speak in a monstrous little voice. *I, ii, 55*

I am slow of study. *I, ii, 70*

That would hang us, every mother's son. *I, ii, 81*

I will aggravate my voice so that I will roar you as
gently as any sucking dove; I will roar you as 'twere
any nightingale. *I, ii,* 85

A proper man, as one shall see in a summer's day; a
most lovely, gentleman-like man. *I, ii,* 89

Over hill, over dale,
Thorough bush, thorough brier,
Over park, over pale,
Thorough flood, thorough fire. *II, i,* 2

I must go seek some dew drops here,
And hang a pearl in every cowslip's ear. *II, i,* 14

I am that merry wanderer of the night.
I jest to Oberon, and make him smile
When I a fat and bean-fed horse beguile,
Neighing in likeness of a filly foal:
And sometimes lurk I in a gossip's bowl,
In very likeness of a roasted crab. *II, i,* 43

Ill met by moonlight, proud Titania. *II, i,* 60

These are the forgeries of jealousy. *II, i,* 81

Since once I sat upon a promontory,
And heard a mermaid on a dolphin's back
Uttering such dulcet and harmonious breath,
That the rude sea grew civil at her song,
And certain stars shot madly from their spheres
To hear the sea-maid's music. *II, i, 149*

And the imperial votaress passed on,
In maiden meditation, fancy-free.
Yet mark'd I where the bolt of Cupid fell:
It fell upon a little western flower,
Before milk-white, now purple with love's wound,
And maidens call it, Love-in-idleness. *II, i, 163*

I'll put a girdle round about the earth
In forty minutes. *II, i, 175*

For you in my respect are all the world:
Then how can it be said I am alone,
When all the world is here to look on me?
II, i, 224

I know a bank whereon the wild thyme blows,
Where oxlips and the nodding violet grows
Quite over-canopied with luscious woodbine,
With sweet musk-roses, and with eglantine:
There sleeps Titania some time of the night,

Lull'd in these flowers with dances and delight;
And there the snake throws her enamell'd skin,
Weed wide enough to wrap a fairy in.   *II, i,* 249

Some to kill cankers in the musk-rose buds,
Some war with rere-mice for their leathern wings,
To make my small elves coats.   *II, ii,* 3

The clamorous owl, that nightly hoots, and wonders
At our quaint spirits.   *II, ii,* 6

You spotted snakes with double tongue,
Thorny hedge-hogs, be not seen;
Newts, and blind-worms, do no wrong;
Come not near our fairy queen.   *II, ii,* 9

Night and silence! who is here?
Weeds of Athens he doth wear.   *II, ii,* 70

As a surfeit of the sweetest things
The deepest loathing to the stomach brings.   *II, ii,* 137

To bring in — God shield us! — a lion among ladies,
is a most dreadful thing; for there is not a more fearful
wild-fowl than your lion living.   *III, i,* 32

A calendar, a calendar! look in the almanack; find out
moonshine. *III, i, 55*

Bless thee, Bottom! bless thee! thou art translated.
III, i, 124

Lord, what fools these mortals be! *III, ii, 115*

So we grew together,
Like to a double cherry, seeming parted,
But yet an union in partition;
Two lovely berries molded on one stem. *III, ii, 208*

Though she be but little, she is fierce. *III, ii, 325*

I have a reasonable good ear in music: let us have the
tongs and the bones. *IV, i, 32*

Truly, a peck of provender: I could munch your good
dry oats. Methinks I have a great desire to a bottle of
hay: good hay, sweet hay, hath no fellow. *IV, i, 36*

I have an exposition of sleep come upon me. *IV, i, 44*

My Oberon! what visions have I seen!
Methought I was enamor'd of an ass. *IV, i,* 82

I never heard
So musical a discord, such sweet thunder. *IV, i,* 123

I have had a dream, past the wit of man to say what
dream it was. *IV, i,* 211

The eye of man hath not heard, the ear of man hath
not seen, man's hand is not able to taste, his tongue to
conceive, nor his heart to report, what my dream was.
IV, i, 218

Eat no onions nor garlic, for we are to utter sweet
breath. *IV, ii,* 44

The lunatic, the lover, and the poet,
Are of imagination all compact:
One sees more devils than vast hell can hold,
That is, the madman; the lover, all as frantic,
Sees Helen's beauty in a brow of Egypt:
The poet's eye, in a fine frenzy rolling,
Doth glance from heaven to earth, from earth to heaven;
And, as imagination bodies forth
The forms of things unknown, the poet's pen
Turns them to shapes, and gives to airy nothing

A local habitation and a name.
Such tricks hath strong imagination,
That, if it would but apprehend some joy,
It comprehends some bringer of that joy;
Or in the night, imagining some fear,
How easy is a bush suppos'd a bear! *V, i,* 7

But all the story of the night told over,
And all their minds transfigur'd so together,
More witnesseth than fancy's images,
And grows to something of great constancy,
But, howsoever, strange and admirable. *V, i,* 23

Very tragical mirth. *V, i,* 57

The true beginning of our end. *V, i,* 111

The best in this kind are but shadows. *V, i,* 215

A very gentle beast, and of a good conscience. *V, i,* 232

All that I have to say, is, to tell you that the lanthorn
is the moon; I, the man in the moon; this thorn-bush,
my thorn-bush; and this dog, my dog. *V, i,* 263

Well roared, Lion. *V, i, 272*

This passion, and the death of a dear friend, would go
near to make a man look sad. *V, i, 295*

With the help of a surgeon, he might yet recover, and
prove an ass. *V, i, 318*

No epilogue, I pray you, for your play needs no
excuse. Never excuse. *V, i, 363*

The iron tongue of midnight hath told twelve;
Lovers, to bed; 'tis almost fairy time. *V, i, 372*

If we shadows have offended,
Think but this, and all is mended,
That you have but slumber'd here
While these visions did appear. *V, ii, 54*

ROMEO AND JULIET [1595–1596]

A pair of star-cross'd lovers. *Prologue, l. 6*

Saint-seducing gold. *Act I, sc. i, l. 220*

One fire burns out another's burning,
One pain is lessen'd by another's anguish. *I, ii, 47*

I will make thee think thy swan a crow. *I, ii, 92*

For I am proverb'd with a grandsire phrase. *I, iv, 37*

We burn daylight. *I, iv, 43*

O! then, I see, Queen Mab hath been with you! . . .
She is the fairies' midwife, and she comes
In shape no bigger than an agate-stone
On the forefinger of an alderman,
Drawn with a team of little atomies
Athwart men's noses as they lie asleep. *I, iv, 53*

True, I talk of dreams,
Which are the children of an idle brain,
Begot of nothing but vain fantasy. *I, iv, 97*

For you and I are past our dancing days. *I, v, 35*

It seems she hangs upon the cheek of night
Like a rich jewel in an Ethiop's ear;
Beauty too rich for use, for earth too dear! *I, v, 49*

My only love sprung from my only hate!
Too early seen unknown, and known too late! *I, v, 142*

Young Adam Cupid, he that shot so trim
When King Cophetua lov'd the beggarmaid. *II, i, 13*

He jests at scars, that never felt a wound.
But, soft! what light through yonder window breaks?
It is the east, and Juliet is the sun! *II, ii, 1*

She speaks, yet she says nothing. *II, ii, 12*

See! how she leans her cheek upon her hand:
O! that I were a glove upon that hand,
That I might touch that cheek. *II, ii, 23*

O Romeo, Romeo! wherefore art thou Romeo?
Deny thy father, and refuse thy name;
Or, if thou wilt not, be but sworn my love,
And I'll no longer be a Capulet. *II, ii, 33*

What's in a name? that which we call a rose
By any other name would smell as sweet. *II, ii, 43*

For stony limits cannot hold love out. *II, ii, 67*

At lovers' perjuries,
They say, Jove laughs. *II, ii, 92*

In truth, fair Montague, I am too fond. *II, ii, 98*

I'll prove more true
Than those that have more cunning to be strange.
II, ii, 100

Romeo: Lady, by yonder blessed moon I swear
That tips with silver all these fruit-tree tops —
Juliet: O! swear not by the moon, the inconstant moon,
That monthly changes in her circled orb,
Lest that thy love prove likewise variable. *II, ii, 107*

Do not swear at all;
Or, if thou wilt, swear by thy gracious self,
Which is the god of my idolatry. *II, ii, 112*

It is too rash, too unadvis'd, too sudden;
Too like the lightning, which doth cease to be
Ere one can say it lightens. *II, ii, 118*

This bud of love, by summer's ripening breath,
May prove a beauteous flower when next we meet.
II, ii, 121

Love goes toward love, as schoolboys from their books;
But love from love, toward school with heavy looks.
II, ii, 156

O! for a falconer's voice,
To lure this tassel-gentle back again. *II, ii, 158*

How silver-sweet sound lovers' tongues by night,
Like softest music to attending ears! *II, ii, 165*

I would have thee gone;
And yet no further than a wanton's bird,
Who lets it hop a little from her hand,
Like a poor prisoner in his twisted gyves,
And with a silk thread plucks it back again,
So loving-jealous of his liberty. *II, ii, 176*

Good night, good night! parting is such sweet sorrow,
That I shall say good night till it be morrow. *II, ii, 184*

Virtue itself turns vice, being misapplied;
And vice sometime's by action dignified. *II, iii, 21*

Care keeps his watch in every old man's eye,
And where care lodges, sleep will never lie. *II, iii, 35*

Wisely and slow; they stumble that run fast. *II, iii, 94*

One, two, and the third in your bosom. *II, iv, 24*

O flesh, flesh, how art thou fishified! *II, iv, 41*

The very pink of courtesy. *II, iv, 63*

A gentleman, nurse, that loves to hear himself talk,
and will speak more in a minute than he will stand to
in a month. *II, iv, 156*

These violent delights have violent ends. *II, vi, 9*

Therefore love moderately; long love doth so;
Too swift arrives as tardy as too slow. *II, vi, 14*

Thy head is as full of quarrels as an egg is full of meat.
III, i, 23

A word and a blow. *III, i, 44*

No, 'tis not so deep as a well, nor so wide as a church
door; but 'tis enough, 'twill serve: ask for me
tomorrow, and you shall find me a grave man. *III, i, 101*

A plague o' both your houses!
They have made worms' meat of me. *III, i, 112*

O! I am Fortune's fool. *III, i, 142*

Gallop apace, you fiery-footed steeds,
Towards Phoebus' lodging. *III, ii, 1*

When he shall die,
Take him and cut him out in little stars,
And he will make the face of heaven so fine
That all the world will be in love with night,
And pay no worship to the garish sun. *III, ii, 21*

He was not born to shame:
Upon his brow shame is asham'd to sit. *III, ii, 91*

Adversity's sweet milk, philosophy. *III, iii, 54*

Hang up philosophy!
Unless philosophy can make a Juliet. *III, iii, 56*

The lark, the herald of the morn. *III, v, 6*

Night's candles are burnt out, and jocund day
Stands tiptoe on the misty mountaintops. *III, v, 9*

Thank me no thankings, nor proud me no prouds.
III, v, 153

Is there no pity sitting in the clouds,
That sees into the bottom of my grief? *III, v, 198*

Past hope, past cure, past help! *IV, i, 45*

'Tis an ill cook that cannot lick his own fingers. *IV, ii, 6*

Apothecary: My poverty, but not my will, consents.
Romeo: I pay thy poverty, and not thy will. *V, i, 75*

The strength
Of twenty men. *V, i, 78*

The time and my intents are savage-wild,
More fierce and more inexorable far
Than empty tigers or the roaring sea. *V, iii, 39*

Tempt not a desperate man. *V, iii, 59*

One writ with me in sour misfortune's book. *V, iii, 82*

How oft when men are at the point of death
Have they been merry! *V, iii, 88*

Beauty's ensign yet
Is crimson in thy lips and in thy cheeks,
And death's pale flag is not advanced there. *V, iii, 94*

O! here
Will I set up my everlasting rest,
And shake the yoke of inauspicious stars
From this world-wearied flesh. Eyes, look your last!
Arms, take your last embrace! *V, iii, 109*

O true apothecary!
Thy drugs are quick. *V, iii, 119*

See what a scourge is laid upon your hate,
That heaven finds means to kill your joys with love.
V, iii, 292

For never was a story of more woe
Than this of Juliet and her Romeo.   *V, iii, 309*

KING HENRY THE FOURTH, PART I [1596–1597]

So shaken as we are, so wan with care.   *Act I, sc. i, l. 1*

In those holy fields
Over whose acres walk'd those blessed feet
Which fourteen hundred years ago were nail'd
For our advantage on the bitter cross.   *I, i, 24*

Unless hours were cups of sack, and minutes capons,
and clocks the tongues of bawds, and dials the signs
of leaping-houses, and the blessed sun himself a fair
hot wench in flame-color'd taffeta, I see no reason
why thou shouldst be so superfluous to demand the
time of the day.   *I, ii, 7*

Diana's foresters, gentlemen of the shade, minions of
the moon.   *I, ii, 29*

A purse of gold most resolutely snatched on Monday
night and most dissolutely spent on Tuesday morning.
I, ii, 38

Thy quips and thy quiddities. *I, ii, 51*

So far as my coin would stretch; and where it would
not, I have used my credit. *I, ii, 61*

Old father antick the law. *I, ii, 69*

I am as melancholy as a gib cat, or a lugged bear.
I, ii, 82

I would to God thou and I knew where a commodity
of good names were to be bought. *I, ii, 92*

O! thou hast damnable iteration, and art indeed able
to corrupt a saint. *I, ii, 101*

Now am I, if a man should speak truly, little better
than one of the wicked. *I, ii, 105*

'Tis my vocation, Hal; 'tis no sin for a man to labor in
his vocation. *I, ii, 116*

There's neither honesty, manhood, nor good
fellowship in thee. *I, ii, 154*

Well then, once in my days I'll be a madcap. *I, ii, 158*

I know you all, and will a while uphold
The unyok'd humor of your idleness:
Yet herein will I imitate the sun,
Who doth permit the base contagious clouds
To smother up his beauty from the world,
That when he please again to be himself,
Being wanted, he may be more wonder'd at,
By breaking through the foul and ugly mists
Of vapors that did seem to strangle him.
If all the year were playing holidays,
To sport would be as tedious as to work. *I, ii, 217*

You tread upon my patience. *I, iii, 4*

Came there a certain lord, neat, and trimly dress'd,
Fresh as a bridegroom; and his chin new-reap'd,
Show'd like a stubble-land at harvest-home:
He was perfumed like a milliner,
And 'twixt his finger and his thumb he held
A pouncet-box, which ever and anon
He gave his nose and took 't away again. *I, iii, 33*

And as the soldiers bore dead bodies by,
He call'd them untaught knaves, unmannerly,
To bring a slovenly unhandsome corpse
Betwixt the wind and his nobility. *I, iii, 42*

So pester'd with a popinjay. *I, iii, 50*

God save the mark! *I, iii, 56*

To put down Richard, that sweet lovely rose,
And plant this thorn, this canker, Bolingbroke. *I, iii, 176*

Or sink or swim. *I, iii, 194*

O! the blood more stirs
To rouse a lion than to start a hare! *I, iii, 197*

By heaven methinks it were an easy leap
To pluck bright honor from the pale-fac'd moon,
Or dive into the bottom of the deep,
Where fathom-line could never touch the ground,
And pluck up drowned honor by the locks. *I, iii, 201*

Why, what a candy deal of courtesy
This fawning greyhound then did proffer me! *I, iii, 251*

I know a trick worth two of that. *II, i, 40*

If the rascal have not given me medicines to make me
love him, I'll be hanged. *II, ii, 20*

I'll starve ere I'll rob a foot further. *II, ii, 24*

It would be argument for a week, laughter for a
month, and a good jest forever. *II, ii, 104*

Falstaff sweats to death
And lards the lean earth as he walks along. *II, ii, 119*

Out of this nettle, danger, we pluck this flower, safety.
II, iii, 11

I could brain him with his lady's fan. *II, iii, 26*

Constant you are,
But yet a woman: and for secrecy,
No lady closer; for I well believe
Thou wilt not utter what thou dost not know;
And so far will I trust thee, gentle Kate. *II, iii, 113*

A Corinthian, a lad of mettle, a good boy. *II, iv, 13*

I am not yet of Percy's mind, the Hotspur of the
North; he that kills me some six or seven dozen of
Scots at a breakfast, washes his hands, and says to his
wife, "Fie upon this quiet life! I want work." *II, iv, 116*

A plague of all cowards, I say. *II, iv, 129*

There live not three good men unhanged in England,
and one of them is fat and grows old. *II, iv, 146*

You care not who sees your back: call you that
backing of your friends? A plague upon such backing!
II, iv, 168

I have peppered two of them. . . . I tell thee what, Hal, if
I tell thee a lie, spit in my face, call me horse. *II, iv, 216*

Give you a reason on compulsion! if reasons were as
plenty as blackberries, I would give no man a reason
upon compulsion, I. *II, iv, 267*

Mark now, how a plain tale shall put you down.
II, iv, 285

What doth gravity out of his bed at midnight? *II, iv, 328*

A plague of sighing and grief! it blows a man up like a
bladder. *II, iv,* 370

I must speak in passion, and I will do it in King
Cambyses' vein. *II, iv,* 429

That reverend vice, that gray iniquity, that father
ruffian, that vanity in years. *II, iv,* 505

If sack and sugar be a fault, God help the wicked! If to
be old and merry be a sin, then many an old host that
I know is damned: if to be fat be to be hated, then
Pharaoh's lean kine are to be loved. *II, iv,* 524

Banish plump Jack, and banish all the world. *II, iv,* 534

Play out the play. *II, iv,* 539

O, monstrous! but one half-penny-worth of bread to
this intolerable deal of sack! *II, iv,* 597

Diseased nature oftentimes breaks forth
In strange eruptions. *III, i,* 27

I am not in the roll of common men. *III, i,* 43

Glendower: I can call spirits from the vasty deep.
Hotspur: Why, so can I, or so can any man;
But will they come when you do call for them? *III, i, 53*

I had rather be a kitten and cry mew,
Than one of these same meter ballad-mongers.
III, i, 128

Mincing poetry:
'Tis like the forc'd gait of a shuffling nag. *III, i, 133*

But in the way of bargain, mark you me,
I'll cavil on the ninth part of a hair. *III, i, 138*

A deal of skimble-skamble stuff. *III, i, 153*

I understand thy kisses and thou mine,
And that's a feeling disputation. *III, i, 204*

Lady Percy: . . . Lie still, ye thief, and hear the lady
sing in Welsh.
Hotspur: I had rather hear Lady, my brach, howl in
Irish. *III, i, 238*

A good mouth-filling oath. *III, i, 258*

They surfeited with honey and began
To loathe the taste of sweetness, whereof a little
More than a little is by much too much. *III, ii, 71*

He was but as the cuckoo is in June,
Heard, not regarded. *III, ii, 75*

My near'st and dearest enemy. *III, ii, 123*

The end of life cancels all bands. *III, ii, 157*

An I have not forgotten what the inside of a church is
made of, I am a peppercorn, a brewer's horse. *III, iii, 8*

Company, villanous company, hath been the spoil
of me. *III, iii, 10*

I have more flesh than another man, and therefore
more frailty. *III, iii, 187*

The very life-blood of our enterprise. *IV, i, 28*

Were it good
To set the exact wealth of all our states
All at one cast? to set so rich a main
On the nice hazard of one doubtful hour? *IV, i, 45*

Baited like eagles having lately bath'd . . .
As full of spirit as the month of May,
And gorgeous as the sun at midsummer. *IV, i, 99*

I saw young Harry, with his beaver on. *IV, i, 104*

To turn and wind a fiery Pegasus
And witch the world with noble horsemanship.
IV, i, 109

Worse than the sun in March
This praise doth nourish agues. *IV, i, 111*

Doomsday is near; die all, die merrily. *IV, i, 134*

The cankers of a calm world and a long peace. *IV, ii, 32*

Tut, tut, good enough to toss; food for powder, food
for powder; they'll fill a pit as well as better. *IV, ii, 72*

Suspicion all our lives shall be stuck full of eyes;
For treason is but trusted like the fox. *V, ii,* 8

Let me tell the world. *V, ii,* 65

The time of life is short;
To spend that shortness basely were too long. *V, ii,* 81

Two stars keep not their motion in one sphere. *V, iv,* 65

But thought's the slave of life, and life time's fool;
And time, that takes survey of all the world,
Must have a stop. O! I could prophesy,
But that the earthy and cold hand of death
Lies on my tongue. *V, iv,* 81

This earth, that bears thee dead,
Bears not alive so stout a gentleman. *V, iv,* 92

Thy ignominy sleep with thee in the grave,
But not remember'd in thy epitaph! *V, iv,* 100

I could have better spar'd a better man. *V, iv,* 104

The better part of valor is discretion. *V, iv,* 120

To the latter end of a fray and the beginning of a feast
Fits a dull fighter and a keen guest. *IV, ii, 86*

Greatness knows itself. *IV, iii, 74*

I could be well content
To entertain the lag-end of my life
With quiet hours. *V, i, 23*

Rebellion lay in his way, and he found it. *V, i, 28*

Never yet did insurrection want
Such water-colors to impaint his cause. *V, i, 79*

I would it were bed-time, Hal, and all well. *V, i, 126*

Honor pricks me on. Yea, but how if honor prick me
off when I come on? how then? Can honor set to a
leg? No. Or an arm? No. Or take away the grief of a
wound? No. Honor hath no skill in surgery then? No.
What is honor? a word. What is that word, honor?
Air. A trim reckoning! Who hath it? he that died o'
Wednesday. Doth he feel it? No. Doth he hear it? No.
It is insensible then? Yea, to the dead. But will it not
live with the living? No. Why? Detraction will not
suffer it. Therefore I'll none of it: honor is a mere
scutcheon; and so ends my catechism. *V, i, 131*

Full bravely hast thou flesh'd
Thy maiden sword. *V, iv,* 132

Lord, Lord, how this world is given to lying! *V, iv,* 148

I'll purge, and leave sack, and live cleanly. *V, iv,* 168

THE MERCHANT OF VENICE [1596–1597]

Your mind is tossing on the ocean. *Act I, sc. i, l.* 8

My ventures are not in one bottom trusted,
Nor to one place. *I, i,* 42

Nature hath fram'd strange fellows in her time. *I, i,* 51

You have too much respect upon the world:
They lose it that do buy it with much care. *I, i,* 74

I hold the world but as the world, Gratiano;
A stage where every man must play a part,
And mine a sad one. *I, i,* 77

Why should a man, whose blood is warm within,
Sit like his grandsire cut in alabaster? *I, i, 83*

There are a sort of men whose visages
Do cream and mantle like a standing pond. *I, i, 88*

I am Sir Oracle,
And when I ope my lips let no dog bark! *I, i, 93*

I do know of these,
That therefore only are reputed wise
For saying nothing. *I, i, 95*

Fish not, with this melancholy bait,
For this fool-gudgeon, this opinion. *I, i, 101*

Gratiano speaks an infinite deal of nothing, more than
any man in all Venice. His reasons are as two grains of
wheat hid in two bushels of chaff: you shall seek all
day ere you find them, and, when you have them,
they are not worth the search. *I, i, 114*

In my school-days, when I had lost one shaft,
I shot his fellow of the selfsame flight
The selfsame way with more advised watch,
To find the other forth, and by adventuring both,
I oft found both. *I, i, 141*

They are as sick that surfeit with too much as they
that starve with nothing. *I, ii, 5*

Superfluity comes sooner by white hairs, but
competency lives longer. *I, ii, 9*

If to do were as easy as to know what were good to
do, chapels had been churches, and poor men's
cottages princes' palaces. *I, ii, 13*

The brain may devise laws for the blood, but a hot
temper leaps o'er a cold decree. *I, ii, 19*

He doth nothing but talk of his horse. *I, ii, 43*

I fear he will prove the weeping philosopher when he
grows old, being so full of unmannerly sadness in his
youth. *I, ii, 51*

God made him, and therefore let him pass for a man.
I, ii, 59

When he is best, he is a little worse than a man, and
when he is worst, he is little better than a beast.
I, ii, 93

I dote on his very absence. *I, ii, 118*

Ships are but boards, sailors but men: there be
land-rats and water-rats, land-thieves and
water-thieves. *I, iii, 22*

Yes, to smell pork; to eat of the habitation which
your prophet the Nazarite conjured the devil into. I
will buy with you, sell with you, talk with you, walk
with you, and so following; but I will not eat with
you, drink with you, nor pray with you. What news
on the Rialto? *I, iii, 34*

How like a fawning publican he looks!
I hate him for he is a Christian. *I, iii, 42*

If I can catch him once upon the hip,
I will feed fat the ancient grudge I bear him. *I, iii, 47*

Cursed be my tribe,
If I forgive him! *I, iii, 52*

The devil can cite Scripture for his purpose. *I, iii, 99*

A goodly apple rotten at the heart.
O, what a goodly outside falsehood hath! *I, iii, 102*

For sufferance is the badge of all our tribe.
You call me misbeliever, cut-throat dog,
And spet upon my Jewish gaberdine. *I, iii, 111*

Shall I bend low, and in a bondman's key,
With bated breath, and whispering humbleness,
Say this. *I, iii, 124*

I'll seal to such a bond,
And say there is much kindness in the Jew. *I, iii, 153*

O father Abram! what these Christians are,
Whose own hard dealing teaches them suspect
The thoughts of others. *I, iii, 161*

I like not fair terms and a villain's mind. *I, iii, 180*

Mislike me not for my complexion,
The shadow'd livery of the burnish'd sun.   *II, i, 1*

O heavens! this is my true-begotten father.   *II, ii, 36*

An honest, exceeding poor man.   *II, ii, 54*

The very staff of my age, my very prop.   *II, ii, 71*

It is a wise father that knows his own child.   *II, ii, 83*

And the vile squealing of the wry-neck'd fife.   *II, v, 30*

Who riseth from a feast
With that keen appetite that he sits down?   *II, vi, 8*

But love is blind, and lovers cannot see
The pretty follies that themselves commit.   *II, vi, 36*

Must I hold a candle to my shames?   *II, vi, 41*

Men that hazard all
Do it in hope of fair advantages:
A golden mind stoops not to shows of dross.   *II, vii, 18*

Young in limbs, in judgment old. *II, vii,* 71

My daughter! O my ducats! O my daughter!
Fled with a Christian! O my Christian ducats!
Justice! the law! my ducats, and my daughter!
A sealed bag, two sealed bags of ducats,
Of double ducats, stol'n from me by my daughter!
II, viii, 15

The fool multitude, that choose by show. *II, ix,* 26

I will not jump with common spirits
And rank me with the barbarous multitude. *II, ix,* 32

Let none presume
To wear an undeserved dignity.
O! that estates, degrees, and offices
Were not deriv'd corruptly, and that clear honor
Were purchas'd by the merit of the wearer. *II, ix,* 39

Some there be that shadows kiss;
Such have but a shadow's bliss. *II, ix,* 66

Let him look to his bond. *III, i,* 49

I am a Jew. Hath not a Jew eyes? hath not a Jew
hands, organs, dimensions, senses, affections,
passions? *III, i, 62*

If you prick us, do we not bleed? if you tickle us, do
we not laugh? if you poison us, do we not die? and if
you wrong us, shall we not revenge? *III, i, 65*

The villainy you teach me I will execute, and it shall
go hard but I will better the instruction. *III, i, 76*

I would not have given it for a wilderness of monkeys.
III, i, 130

There's something tells me, but it is not love,
I would not lose you; and you know yourself,
Hate counsels not in such a quality. *III, ii, 4*

Makes a swanlike end,
Fading in music. *III, ii, 44*

Tell me where is fancy bred,
Or in the heart or in the head?
How begot, how nourished?
Reply, reply. *III, ii, 63*

In law, what plea so tainted and corrupt
But, being season'd with a gracious voice,
Obscures the show of evil?   *III, ii, 75*

There is no vice so simple but assumes
Some mark of virtue on his outward parts.   *III, ii, 81*

The seeming truth which cunning times put on
To entrap the wisest.   *III, ii, 100*

How all the other passions fleet to air,
As doubtful thoughts, and rash-embrac'd despair,
And shuddering fear, and green-ey'd jealousy.   *III, ii, 108*

An unlesson'd girl, unschool'd, unpractic'd;
Happy in this, she is not yet so old
But she may learn.   *III, ii, 160*

Here are a few of the unpleasant'st words
That ever blotted paper.   *III, ii, 252*

Thou call'dst me dog before thou hadst a cause,
But, since I am a dog, beware my fangs.   *III, iii, 6*

Thus when I shun Scylla, your father, I fall into
Charybdis, your mother. *III, v, 17*

Some men there are love not a gaping pig;
Some, that are mad if they behold a cat. *IV, i, 47*

A harmless necessary cat. *IV, i, 55*

Bassanio: Do all men kill the things they do not love?
Shylock: Hates any man the thing he would not kill?
IV, i, 66

What! wouldst thou have a serpent sting thee twice?
IV, i, 69

The weakest kind of fruit
Drops earliest to the ground. *IV, i, 115*

To hold opinion with Pythagoras,
That souls of animals infuse themselves
Into the trunks of men. *IV, i, 131*

I never knew so young a body with so old a head.
IV, i, 163

The quality of mercy is not strain'd,
It droppeth as the gentle rain from heaven
Upon the place beneath: it is twice bless'd;
It blesseth him that gives and him that takes:
'Tis mightiest in the mightiest; it becomes
The throned monarch better than his crown;
His scepter shows the force of temporal power,
The attribute to awe and majesty,
Wherein doth sit the dread and fear of kings;
But mercy is above this sceptered sway,
It is enthroned in the hearts of kings,
It is an attribute to God himself,
And earthly power doth then show likest God's
When mercy seasons justice. Therefore, Jew,
Though justice be thy plea, consider this,
That in the course of justice none of us
Should see salvation: we do pray for mercy,
And that same prayer doth teach us all to render
The deeds of mercy. *IV, i,* 184

To do a great right, do a little wrong. *IV, i,* 216

A Daniel come to judgment! yea, a Daniel! *IV, i,* 223

How much more elder art thou than thy looks!
IV, i, 251

Is it so nominated in the bond? *IV, i,* 260

'Tis not in the bond. *IV, i,* 263

For herein Fortune shows herself more kind
Than is her custom: it is still her use
To let the wretched man outlive his wealth,
To view with hollow eye and wrinkled brow
An age of poverty. *IV, i,* 268

I have a daughter;
Would any of the stock of Barabbas
Had been her husband rather than a Christian! *IV, i,* 296

An upright judge, a learned judge! *IV, i,* 324

Now, infidel, I have thee on the hip. *IV, i,* 334

A Daniel, still say I; a second Daniel!
I thank thee, Jew, for teaching me that word. *IV, i,* 341

You take my house when you do take the prop
That doth sustain my house; you take my life
When you do take the means whereby I live. *IV, i,* 376

He is well paid that is well satisfied. *IV, i, 416*

Lorenzo: The moon shines bright: in such a night
as this . . .
Troilus methinks mounted the Troyan walls,
And sigh'd his soul toward the Grecian tents,
Where Cressid lay that night.
Jessica: In such a night
Did Thisbe fearfully o'ertrip the dew,
And saw the lion's shadow ere himself,
And ran dismay'd away.
Lorenzo: In such a night
Stood Dido with a willow in her hand
Upon the wild sea-banks, and waft her love
To come again to Carthage.
Jessica: In such a night
Medea gather'd the enchanted herbs
That did renew old Aeson. *V, i, 1*

How sweet the moonlight sleeps upon this bank!
Here we will sit, and let the sounds of music
Creep in our ears: soft stillness and the night
Become the touches of sweet harmony.
Sit, Jessica: look, how the floor of heaven
Is thick inlaid with patines of bright gold:
There's not the smallest orb which thou behold'st
But in his motion like an angel sings,
Still quiring to the young-eyed cherubins.

Such harmony is in immortal souls;
But, whilst this muddy vesture of decay
Doth grossly close it in, we cannot hear it. *V, i, 54*

I am never merry when I hear sweet music. *V, i, 69*

The man that hath no music in himself,
Nor is not mov'd with concord of sweet sounds,
Is fit for treasons, stratagems, and spoils;
The motions of his spirit are dull as night,
And his affections dark as Erebus:
Let no such man be trusted. *V, i, 83*

How far that little candle throws his beams!
So shines a good deed in a naughty world. *V, i, 90*

How many things by season season'd are
To their right praise and true perfection! *V, i, 107*

This night methinks is but the daylight sick. *V, i, 124*

A light wife doth make a heavy husband. *V, i, 130*

These blessed candles of the night. *V, i, 220*

THE MERRY WIVES OF WINDSOR [1597, revised 1600–1601]

I will make a Star Chamber matter of it. *Act I, sc. i, l. 2*

She has brown hair, and speaks small like a woman.
I, i, 48

Seven hundred pounds and possibilities is goot gifts.
I, i, 65

I had rather than forty shillings I had my Book of
Songs and Sonnets here. *I, i, 205*

"Convey," the wise it call. "Steal" foh! a fico for the
phrase! *I, iii, 30*

I am almost out at heels. *I, iii, 32*

Thou art the Mars of malcontents. *I, iii, 111*

Here will be an old abusing of God's patience and the
king's English. *I, iv, 5*

Dispense with trifles. *II, i, 47*

Faith, thou hast some crotchets in thy head now.
II, i, 158

Why, then the world's mine oyster,
Which I with sword will open. *II, ii, 2*

This is the short and the long of it. *II, ii, 62*

Like a fair house built upon another man's ground.
II, ii, 229

Better three hours too soon than a minute too late.
II, ii, 332

I cannot tell what the dickens his name is. *III, ii, 20*

He capers, he dances, he has eyes of youth, he writes
verses, he speaks holiday, he smells April and May.
III, ii, 71

O, what a world of vile ill-favor'd faults
Looks handsome in three hundred pounds a year!
III, iv, 32

A woman would run through fire and water for such a kind heart. *III, iv, 106*

I have a kind of alacrity in sinking. *III, v, 13*

As good luck would have it. *III, v, 86*

A man of my kidney. *III, v, 119*

[He] curses all Eve's daughters, of what complexion soever. *IV, ii, 24*

Wives may be merry, and yet honest too. *IV, ii, 110*

This is the third time; I hope good luck lies in odd numbers. . . . There is divinity in odd numbers, either in nativity, chance or death. *V, i, 2*

Better a little chiding than a great deal of heartbreak.
V, iii, 10

KING HENRY THE FOURTH, PART II [1598]

Rumor is a pipe
Blown by surmises, jealousies, conjectures,
And of so easy and so plain a stop
That the blunt monster with uncounted heads,
The still-discordant wavering multitude,
Can play upon it. *Induction, l. 15*

Even such a man, so faint, so spiritless,
So dull, so dead in look, so woe-begone,
Drew Priam's curtain in the dead of night,
And would have told him half his Troy was burn'd.
Act I, sc. i, l. 70

Yet the first bringer of unwelcome news
Hath but a losing office, and his tongue
Sounds ever after as a sullen bell,
Remember'd knolling a departing friend. *I, i, 100*

I am not only witty in myself, but the cause that wit is
in other men. *I, ii, 10*

A rascally yea-forsooth knave. *I, ii, 40*

You lie in your throat. *I, ii, 97*

Your lordship, though not clean past your youth, hath
yet some smack of age in you, some relish of the
saltness of time. *I, ii, 112*

It is the disease of not listening, the malady of not
marking, that I am troubled withal. *I, ii, 139*

I am as poor as Job, my lord, but not so patient.
I, ii, 145

We that are in the vaward of our youth. *I, ii, 201*

Have you not a moist eye, a dry hand, a yellow cheek,
a white beard, a decreasing leg, an increasing belly?
I, ii, 206

Every part about you blasted with antiquity. *I, ii, 210*

For my voice, I have lost it with hollaing and singing
of anthems. *I, ii, 215*

It was always yet the trick of our English nation, if
they have a good thing, to make it too common.
I, ii, 244

I were better to be eaten to death with rust than to be
scoured to nothing with perpetual motion. *I, ii, 249*

I can get no remedy against this consumption of the
purse: borrowing only lingers and lingers it out, but
the disease is incurable. *I, ii, 267*

Who lin'd himself with hope,
Eating the air on promise of supply. *I, iii, 27*

A habitation giddy and unsure
Hath he that buildeth on the vulgar heart. *I, iii, 89*

Past and to come seem best; things present worst.
I, iii, 108

A poor lone woman. *II, i, 37*

Away, you scullion! you rampallian! you fustilarian! I'll
tickle your catastrophe. *II, i, 67*

He hath eaten me out of house and home. *II, i, 82*

Let the end try the man. *II, ii, 52*

Thus we play the fools with the time, and the spirits
of the wise sit in the clouds and mock us. *II, ii, 155*

He was indeed the glass
Wherein the noble youth did dress themselves.
II, iii, 21

And let the welkin roar. *II, iv, 181*

Is it not strange that desire should so many years
outlive performance? *II, iv, 283*

O sleep! O gentle sleep!
Nature's soft nurse, how have I frighted thee,
That thou no more wilt weigh my eyelids down
And steep my senses in forgetfulness? *III, i, 5*

With all appliances and means to boot. *III, i, 29*

Uneasy lies the head that wears a crown. *III, i, 31*

O God! that one might read the book of fate. *III, i,* 45

There is a history in all men's lives. *III, i,* 80

Death, as the Psalmist saith, is certain to all;
all shall die. *III, ii,* 41

We have heard the chimes at midnight. *III, ii,* 231

A man can die but once; we owe God a death.
III, ii, 253

We see which way the stream of time doth run
And are enforc'd from our most quiet sphere
By the rough torrent of occasion. *IV, i,* 70

We ready are to try our fortunes
To the last man. *IV, ii,* 43

I may justly say with the hook-nosed fellow of Rome,
"I came, saw, and overcame." *IV, iii,* 44

O polish'd perturbation! golden care!
That keep'st the ports of slumber open wide
To many a watchful night! *IV, v,* 22

See, sons, what things you are!
How quickly nature falls into revolt
When gold becomes her object! *IV, v, 63*

Thy wish was father, Harry, to that thought! *IV, v, 91*

Before thy hour be ripe. *IV, v, 95*

Commit
The oldest sins the newest kind of ways. *IV, v, 124*

His cares are now all ended. *V, ii, 3*

This is the English, not the Turkish court;
Not Amurath an Amurath succeeds,
But Harry Harry. *V, ii, 47*

I know thee not, old man: fall to thy prayers;
How ill white hairs become a fool and jester! *V, v, 52*

Master Shallow, I owe you a thousand pound. *V, v, 78*

KING HENRY THE FIFTH [1598–1599]

O! for a Muse of fire, that would ascend
The brightest heaven of invention! *Chorus, l. 1*

Or may we cram
Within this wooden O the very casques
That did affright the air at Agincourt? *Chorus, l. 12*

Consideration like an angel came,
And whipp'd the offending Adam out of him.
Act I, sc. i, l. 28

Hear him debate of commonwealth affairs,
You would say it hath been all in all his study. *I, i, 41*

Turn him to any cause of policy,
The Gordian knot of it he will unloose,
Familiar as his garter; that, when he speaks,
The air, a charter'd libertine, is still. *I, i, 45*

Therefore doth heaven divide
The state of man in divers functions,
Setting endeavor in continual motion;
To which is fixed, as an aim or butt,
Obedience: for so work the honeybees,

Creatures that by a rule in nature teach
The act of order to a peopled kingdom. *I, ii,* 183

The singing masons building roofs of gold. *I, ii,* 198

Many things, having full reference
To one consent, may work contrariously;
As many arrows, loosed several ways,
Fly to one mark; as many ways meet in one town;
As many fresh streams meet in one salt sea;
As many lines close in the dial's center;
So may a thousand actions, once afoot,
End in one purpose, and be all well borne
Without defeat. *I, ii,* 205

'Tis ever common
That men are merriest when they are from home.
I, ii, 271

Now all the youth of England are on fire,
And silken dalliance in the wardrobe lies. *II, Chorus,* 1

O England! model to thy inward greatness,
Like little body with a mighty heart,
What mightst thou do, that honor would thee do,
Were all thy children kind and natural! *II, Chorus,* 16

That's the humor of it. *II, i, 63*

He's [Falstaff's] in Arthur's bosom, if ever man went to
Arthur's bosom. A' made a finer end and went away an
it had been any christom child; a' parted even just
between twelve and one, even at the turning o' the
tide: for after I saw him fumble with the sheets and
play with flowers and smile upon his fingers' ends, I
knew there was but one way; for his nose was as sharp
as a pen, and a' babbled of green fields. *II, iii, 11*

As cold as any stone. *II, iii, 26*

Trust none;
For oaths are straws, men's faiths are wafer-cakes,
And hold-fast is the only dog, my duck. *II, iii, 53*

Once more unto the breach, dear friends, once more;
Or close the wall up with our English dead!
In peace there's nothing so becomes a man
As modest stillness and humility:
But when the blast of war blows in our ears,
Then imitate the action of the tiger;
Stiffen the sinews, summon up the blood,
Disguise fair nature with hard-favor'd rage;
Then lend the eye a terrible aspect. *III, i, 1*

And sheath'd their swords for lack of argument. *III, i,* 21

I see you stand like greyhounds in the slips,
Straining upon the start. The game's afoot:
Follow your spirit; and, upon this charge
Cry "God for Harry! England and Saint George!"
III, i, 31

I would give all my fame for a pot of ale, and safety.
III, ii, 14

Men of few words are the best men. *III, ii,* 40

He will maintain his argument as well as any military
man in the world. *III, ii,* 89

I know the disciplines of wars. *III, ii,* 156

I thought upon one pair of English legs
Did march three Frenchmen. *III, vi,* 161

We are in God's hand. *III, vi,* 181

That island of England breeds very valiant creatures:
their mastiffs are of unmatchable courage. *III, vii,* 155

Give them great meals of beef and iron and steel, they
will eat like wolves and fight like devils. *III, vii, 166*

The hum of either army stilly sounds,
That the fix'd sentinels almost receive
The secret whispers of each other's watch:
Fire answers fire, and through their paly flames
Each battle sees the other's umber'd face:
Steed threatens steed, in high and boastful neighs
Piercing the night's dull ear; and from the tents
The armorers, accomplishing the knights,
With busy hammers closing rivets up,
Give dreadful note of preparation. *IV, Chorus, 5*

A little touch of Harry in the night. *IV, Chorus, 47*

There is some soul of goodness in things evil,
Would men observingly distill it out. *IV, i, 4*

Every subject's duty is the king's; but every subject's
soul is his own. *IV, i, 189*

What infinite heart's ease
Must kings neglect that private men enjoy!
And what have kings that privates have not too,
Save ceremony, save general ceremony?

And what art thou, thou idol ceremony?
What kind of god art thou, that suffer'st more
Of mortal griefs than do thy worshippers?
What are thy rents? what are thy comings-in?
O ceremony! show me but thy worth. *IV, i, 256*

'Tis not the balm, the scepter and the ball,
The sword, the mace, the crown imperial,
The intertissued robe of gold and pearl,
The farced title running 'fore the king,
The throne he sits on, nor the tide of pomp
That beats upon the high shore of this world,
No, not all these, thrice-gorgeous ceremony,
Not all these, laid in bed majestical,
Can sleep so soundly as the wretched slave,
Who with a body fill'd and vacant mind
Gets him to rest, cramm'd with distressful bread.
IV, i, 280

O God of battles! steel my soldiers' hearts;
Possess them not with fear; take from them now
The sense of reckoning, if the opposed numbers
Pluck their hearts from them. *IV, i, 309*

But if it be a sin to covet honor,
I am the most offending soul alive. *IV, iii, 28*

This day is call'd the feast of Crispian:
He that outlives this day, and comes safe home,
Will stand a tip-toe when this day is nam'd.
And rouse him at the name of Crispian. *IV, iii, 40*

We few, we happy few, we band of brothers;
For he today that sheds his blood with me
Shall be my brother. *IV, iii, 60*

The saying is true, "The empty vessel makes the
greatest sound." *IV, iv, 72*

There is occasions and causes why and wherefore in
all things. *V, i, 3*

By this leek, I will most horribly revenge. I eat and
eat, I swear. *V, i, 49*

All hell shall stir for this. *V, i, 72*

The naked, poor, and mangled Peace,
Dear nurse of arts, plenties, and joyful births. *V, ii, 34*

Grow like savages — as soldiers will,
That nothing do but meditate on blood. *V, ii, 59*

For these fellows of infinite tongue, that can rime
themselves into ladies' favors, they do always reason
themselves out again. *V, ii,* 162

My comfort is, that old age, that ill layer-up of beauty,
can do no more spoil upon my face. *V, ii,* 246

O Kate! nice customs curtsy to great kings. *V, ii,* 291

MUCH ADO ABOUT NOTHING [1598–1600]

He hath indeed better bettered expectation than you
must expect of me to tell you how. *Act I, sc. i, l.* 15

How much better is it to weep at joy than to joy at
weeping! *I, i,* 28

A very valiant trencher-man. *I, i,* 52

There's a skirmish of wit between them. *I, i,* 64

He wears his faith but as the fashion of his hat. *I, i,* 76

I see, lady, the gentleman is not in your books. *I, i,* 79

What! my dear Lady Disdain, are you yet living?
I, i, 123

Shall I never see a bachelor of threescore again?
I, i, 209

In time the savage bull doth bear the yoke. *I, i, 271*

Benedick the married man. *I, i, 278*

I could not endure a husband with a beard on his face:
I had rather lie in the woollen. *II, i, 31*

As merry as the day is long. *II, i, 52*

Would it not grieve a woman to be over-mastered
with a piece of valiant dust? to make an account of her
life to a clod of wayward marl? *II, i, 64*

I have a good eye, uncle: I can see a church by
daylight. *II, i, 86*

Speak low, if you speak love. *II, i, 104*

Friendship is constant in all other things
Save in the office and affairs of love:
Therefore all hearts in love use their own tongues;
Let every eye negotiate for itself
And trust no agent. *II, i,* 184

She speaks poniards, and every word stabs: if her
breath were as terrible as her terminations, there were
no living near her; she would infect to the north star.
II, i, 257

Silence is the perfectest herald of joy: I were but little
happy, if I could say how much. *II, i,* 319

It keeps on the windy side of care. *II, i,* 328

There was a star danced, and under that was I born.
II, i, 351

I will tell you my drift. *II, i,* 406

He was wont to speak plain and to the purpose.
II, iii, 19

Sigh no more, ladies, sigh no more.
Men were deceivers ever;
One foot in sea, and one on shore,
To one thing constant never. *II, iii, 65*

Sits the wind in that corner? *II, iii, 108*

Bait the hook well: this fish will bite. *II, iii, 121*

Shall quips and sentences and these paper bullets
of the brain awe a man from the career of his
humor? No; the world must be peopled. When I said
I would die a bachelor, I did not think I should live
till I were married. *II, iii, 260*

From the crown of his head to the sole of his foot, he
is all mirth. *III, ii, 9*

He hath a heart as sound as a bell, and his tongue is
the clapper; for what his heart thinks his tongue
speaks. *III, ii, 12*

Everyone can master a grief but he that has it. *III, ii, 28*

Are you good men and true? *III, iii, 1*

To be a well-favored man is the gift of fortune; but to
write and read comes by nature. *III, iii, 14*

If they make you not then the better answer, you may
say they are not the men you took them for. *III, iii, 49*

The fashion wears out more apparel than the man.
III, iii, 147

A good old man, sir; he will be talking: as they say,
When the age is in, the wit is out. *III, v, 36*

Of what men dare do! what men may do! what men
daily do, not knowing what they do! *IV, i, 19*

O! what authority and show of truth
Can cunning sin cover itself withal. *IV, i, 35*

For it so falls out
That what we have we prize not to the worth
Whiles we enjoy it, but being lack'd and lost,
Why, then we rack the value, then we find
The virtue that possession would not show us
Whiles it was ours. *IV, i, 219*

Masters, it is proved already that you are little better than false knaves, and it will go near to be thought so shortly. *IV, ii, 23*

Flat burglary as ever was committed. *IV, ii, 54*

Thou wilt be condemned into everlasting redemption for this. *IV, ii, 60*

O that he were here to write me down an ass! *IV, ii, 80*

Patch griefs with proverbs. *V, i, 17*

Charm ache with air and agony with words. *V, i, 26*

For there was never yet philosopher
That could endure the toothache patiently. *V, i, 35*

Some of us will smart for it. *V, i, 108*

What though care killed a cat, thou hast mettle enough in thee to kill care. *V, i, 135*

I was not born under a riming planet. *V, ii, 40*

The trumpet of his own virtues. *V, ii, 91*

Done to death by slanderous tongues. *V, iii, 3*

JULIUS CAESAR [1599]

A surgeon to old shoes. *Act I, sc. i, l. 26*

As proper men as ever trod upon neat's leather. *I, i, 27*

Have you not made a universal shout,
That Tiber trembled underneath her banks,
To hear the replication of your sounds
Made in her concave shores? *I, i, 48*

Beware the ides of March. *I, ii, 18*

Set honor in one eye and death i' the other,
And I will look on both indifferently. *I, ii, 86*

Well, honor is the subject of my story.
I cannot tell what you and other men
Think of this life; but, for my single self,
I had as lief not be as live to be
In awe of such a thing as I myself. *I, ii, 92*

Stemming it with hearts of controversy. *I, ii, 109*

Why, man, he doth bestride the narrow world
Like a Colossus; and we petty men
Walk under his huge legs, and peep about
To find ourselves dishonorable graves.
Men at some time are masters of their fates:
The fault, dear Brutus, is not in our stars,
But in ourselves, that we are underlings. *I, ii, 134*

Upon what meat doth this our Caesar feed,
That he is grown so great? *I, ii, 148*

Let me have men about me that are fat;
Sleek-headed men and such as sleep o' nights.
Yond Cassius has a lean and hungry look;
He thinks too much: such men are dangerous. *I, ii, 191*

He reads much;
He is a great observer, and he looks
Quite through the deeds of men. *I, ii, 200*

Seldom he smiles, and smiles in such a sort
As if he mock'd himself, and scorn'd his spirit
That could be mov'd to smile at anything. *I, ii, 204*

But, for my own part, it was Greek to me. *I, ii, 288*

Yesterday the bird of night did sit,
Even at noonday, upon the marketplace,
Hooting and shrieking. *I, iii, 26*

So every bondman in his own hand bears
The power to cancel his captivity. *I, iii, 101*

O! he sits high in all the people's hearts:
And that which would appear offense in us,
His countenance, like richest alchemy,
Will change to virtue and to worthiness. *I, iii, 157*

The abuse of greatness is when it disjoins
Remorse from power. *II, i, 18*

'Tis a common proof,
That lowliness is young ambition's ladder,
Whereto the climber-upward turns his face;
But when he once attains the upmost round,
He then unto the ladder turns his back,
Looks in the clouds, scorning the base degrees
By which he did ascend. *II, i, 21*

Therefore think him as a serpent's egg
Which, hatch'd, would, as his kind, grow mischievous,
And kill him in the shell. *II, i, 32*

Between the acting of a dreadful thing
And the first motion, all the interim is
Like a phantasma, or a hideous dream:
The genius and the mortal instruments
Are then in council; and the state of man,
Like to a little kingdom, suffers then
The nature of an insurrection. *II, i, 63*

O conspiracy!
Sham'st thou to show thy dangerous brow by night,
When evils are most free? *II, i, 77*

Let's carve him as a dish fit for the gods,
Not hew him as a carcass fit for hounds. *II, i, 173*

But when I tell him he hates flatterers,
He says he does, being then most flattered. *II, i, 207*

Enjoy the honey-heavy dew of slumber. *II, i, 230*

Dwell I but in the suburbs
Of your good pleasure? *II, i, 285*

You are my true and honorable wife,
As dear to me as are the ruddy drops
That visit my sad heart. *II, i, 288*

Think you I am no stronger than my sex,
Being so father'd and so husbanded? *II, i, 296*

When beggars die there are no comets seen;
The heavens themselves blaze forth the death of
princes. *II, ii, 30*

Cowards die many times before their deaths;
The valiant never taste of death but once.
Of all the wonders that I yet have heard,
It seems to me most strange that men should fear;
Seeing that death, a necessary end,
Will come when it will come. *II, ii, 32*

Antony, that revels long o' nights. *II, ii, 116*

How hard it is for women to keep counsel! *II, iv, 9*

But I am constant as the northern star,
Of whose true-fix'd and resting quality
There is no fellow in the firmament. *III, i, 60*

Speak, hands, for me! *III, i, 76*

Et tu, Brute? *III, i, 77*

Some to the common pulpits, and cry out,
"Liberty, freedom, and enfranchisement!" *III, i, 79*

How many ages hence
Shall this our lofty scene be acted o'er,
In states unborn and accents yet unknown! *III, i, 111*

O mighty Caesar! dost thou lie so low?
Are all thy conquests, glories, triumphs, spoils,
Shrunk to this little measure? *III, i, 148*

The choice and master spirits of this age. *III, i, 163*

Though last, not least in love. *III, i, 189*

O! pardon me, thou bleeding piece of earth,
That I am meek and gentle with these butchers;
Thou art the ruins of the noblest man
That ever lived in the tide of times. *III, i, 254*

Cry "Havoc!" and let slip the dogs of war. *III, i, 273*

Romans, countrymen, and lovers! hear me for my
cause; and be silent, that you may hear. *III, ii, 13*

Not that I loved Caesar less, but that I loved Rome
more. *III, ii, 22*

As he was valiant, I honor him; but, as he was
ambitious, I slew him. *III, ii, 27*

If any, speak; for him have I offended. I pause for a
reply. *III, ii, 36*

Friends, Romans, countrymen, lend me your ears;
I come to bury Caesar, not to praise him.
The evil that men do lives after them,
The good is oft interred with their bones. *III, ii, 79*

For Brutus is an honorable man;
So are they all, all honorable men.   *III, ii,* 88

When that the poor have cried, Caesar hath wept;
Ambition should be made of sterner stuff.   *III, ii,* 97

O judgment! thou art fled to brutish beasts,
And men have lost their reason.   *III, ii,* 110

But yesterday the word of Caesar might
Have stood against the world; now lies he there,
And none so poor to do him reverence.   *III, ii,* 124

If you have tears, prepare to shed them now.   *III, ii,* 174

See what a rent the envious Casca made.   *III, ii,* 180

This was the most unkindest cut of all.   *III, ii,* 188

Great Caesar fell.
O! what a fall was there, my countrymen;
Then I, and you, and all of us fell down,
Whilst bloody treason flourish'd over us.   *III, ii,* 194

What private griefs they have, alas! I know not.
III, ii, 217

I come not, friends, to steal away your hearts:
I am no orator, as Brutus is;
But, as you know me all, a plain blunt man. *III, ii, 220*

For I have neither wit, nor words, nor worth,
Action, nor utterance, nor the power of speech,
To stir men's blood: I only speak right on. *III, ii, 225*

Put a tongue
In every wound of Caesar, that should move
The stones of Rome to rise and mutiny. *III, ii, 232*

When love begins to sicken and decay,
It useth an enforced ceremony.
There are no tricks in plain and simple faith. *IV, ii, 20*

An itching palm. *IV, iii, 10*

I had rather be a dog, and bay the moon,
Than such a Roman. *IV, iii, 27*

I'll use you for my mirth, yea, for my laughter,
When you are waspish. *IV, iii, 49*

There is no terror, Cassius, in your threats;
For I am arm'd so strong in honesty
That they pass by me as the idle wind,
Which I respect not. *IV, iii, 66*

A friend should bear his friend's infirmities,
But Brutus makes mine greater than they are. *IV, iii, 85*

All his faults observ'd,
Set in a notebook, learn'd, and conn'd by rote. *IV, iii, 96*

There is a tide in the affairs of men,
Which, taken at the flood, leads on to fortune;
Omitted, all the voyage of their life
Is bound in shallows and in miseries. *IV, iii, 217*

We must take the current when it serves,
Or lose our ventures. *IV, iii, 222*

The deep of night is crept upon our talk,
And nature must obey necessity. *IV, iii, 225*

But for your words, they rob the Hybla bees,
   And leave them honeyless. *V, i, 34*

Forever, and forever, farewell, Cassius!
  If we do meet again, why, we shall smile;
If not, why then, this parting was well made. *V, i, 117*

O! that a man might know
The end of this day's business, ere it come. *V, i, 123*

O Julius Caesar! thou art mighty yet!
Thy spirit walks abroad, and turns our swords
   In our own proper entrails. *V, iii, 94*

The last of all the Romans, fare thee well! *V, iii, 99*

This was the noblest Roman of them all. *V, v, 68*

His life was gentle, and the elements
So mix'd in him that Nature might stand up
And say to all the world, "This was a man!" *V, v, 73*

AS YOU LIKE IT [1599–1600]

What's the new news at the new court? *Act I, sc. i, l. 103*

Fleet the time carelessly, as they did in the golden
world. *I, i, 126*

Always the dullness of the fool is the whetstone of
the wits. *I, ii, 59*

The little foolery that wise men have makes a
great show. *I, ii, 97*

Well said: that was laid on with a trowel. *I, ii, 113*

Your heart's desires be with you! *I, ii, 214*

One out of suits with fortune. *I, ii, 263*

My pride fell with my fortunes. *I, ii, 269*

Hereafter, in a better world than this,
I shall desire more love and knowledge of you. *I, ii, 301*

Heavenly Rosalind! *I, ii, 306*

O, how full of briers is this working-day world! *I, iii, 12*

Beauty provoketh thieves sooner than gold. *I, iii, 113*

We'll have a swashing and a martial outside,
As many other mannish cowards have. *I, iii, 123*

Hath not old custom made this life more sweet
Than that of painted pomp? Are not these woods
More free from peril than the envious court? *II, i, 2*

Sweet are the uses of adversity,
Which, like the toad, ugly and venomous,
Wears yet a precious jewel in his head;
And this our life exempt from public haunt,
Finds tongues in trees, books in the running brooks,
Sermons in stones, and good in everything. *II, i, 12*

The big round tears
Cours'd one another down his innocent nose
In piteous chase. *II, i, 38*

Sweep on, you fat and greasy citizens. *II, i, 55*

And He that doth the ravens feed,
Yea, providently caters for the sparrow,
Be comfort to my age! *II, iii, 43*

Though I look old, yet I am strong and lusty;
For in my youth I never did apply
Hot and rebellious liquors in my blood. *II, iii, 47*

Therefore my age is as a lusty winter,
Frosty, but kindly. *II, iii, 52*

Thou art not for the fashion of these times,
Where none will sweat but for promotion. *II, iii, 59*

Ay, now am I in Arden; the more fool I: when I was at
home, I was in a better place: but travelers must be
content. *II, iv, 16*

If you remember'st not the slightest folly
That ever love did make thee run into,
Thou hast not lov'd. *II, iv, 34*

We that are true lovers run into strange capers. *II, iv, 53*

I shall ne'er be ware of mine own wit, till I break my
shins against it. *II, iv, 59*

Under the greenwood tree
Who loves to lie with me,
And turn his merry note
Unto the sweet bird's throat,
Come hither, come hither, come hither:
Here shall he see
No enemy
But winter and rough weather. *II, v, 1*

I can suck melancholy out of a song as a weasel
sucks eggs. *II, v, 12*

Who doth ambition shun,
And loves to live i' the sun,
Seeking the food he eats,
And pleas'd with what he gets. *II, v, 38*

I met a fool i' the forest,
A motley fool. *II, vii, 12*

And then he drew a dial from his poke,
And, looking on it with lack-luster eye,
Says very wisely, "It is ten o'clock;
Thus may we see," quoth he, "how the world wags."
II, vii, 20

And so, from hour to hour we ripe and ripe,
And then from hour to hour we rot and rot,
And thereby hangs a tale. *II, vii,* 26

My lungs began to crow like chanticleer,
That fools should be so deep-contemplative,
And I did laugh sans intermission
An hour by his dial. *II, vii,* 30

Motley's the only wear. *II, vii,* 34

If ladies be but young and fair,
They have the gift to know it. *II, vii,* 37

I must have liberty
Withal, as large a charter as the wind,
To blow on whom I please. *II, vii,* 47

The "why" is plain as way to parish church. *II, vii,* 52

But whate'er you are
That in this desert inaccessible,
Under the shade of melancholy boughs,
Lose and neglect the creeping hours of time;
If ever you have look'd on better days,
If ever been where bells have knoll'd to church,
If ever sat at any good man's feast,
If ever from your eyelids wip'd a tear,
And know what 'tis to pity, and be pitied,
Let gentleness my strong enforcement be. *II, vii,* 109

True is it that we have seen better days. *II, vii,* 120

Oppress'd with two weak evils, age and hunger.
II, vii, 132

All the world's a stage,
And all the men and women merely players:
They have their exits and their entrances;
And one man in his time plays many parts,
His acts being seven ages. At first the infant,
Mewling and puking in the nurse's arms.
And then the whining school-boy, with his satchel,
And shining morning face, creeping like snail
Unwillingly to school. And then the lover,
Sighing like furnace, with a woful ballad
Made to his mistress' eyebrow. Then a soldier,

Full of strange oaths, and bearded like the pard,
Jealous in honor, sudden and quick in quarrel,
Seeking the bubble reputation
Even in the cannon's mouth. And then the justice,
In fair round belly with good capon lin'd,
With eyes severe, and beard of formal cut,
Full of wise saws and modern instances;
And so he plays his part. The sixth age shifts
Into the lean and slipper'd pantaloon,
With spectacles on nose and pouch on side,
His youthful hose well sav'd, a world too wide
For his shrunk shank; and his big manly voice,
Turning again toward childish treble, pipes
And whistles in his sound. Last scene of all,
That ends this strange eventful history,
Is second childishness and mere oblivion,
Sans teeth, sans eyes, sans taste, sans everything.
II, vii, 139

Blow, blow, thou winter wind,
Thou art not so unkind
As man's ingratitude. *II, vii, 174*

These trees shall be my books. *III, ii, 5*

The fair, the chaste, and unexpressive she. *III, ii, 10*

It goes much against my stomach. Hast any
philosophy in thee, shepherd? *III, ii,* 21

He that wants money, means, and content, is without
three good friends. *III, ii,* 25

I am a true laborer: I earn that I eat, get that I wear,
owe no man hate, envy no man's happiness, glad of
other men's good, content with my harm. *III, ii,* 78

From the east to western Ind,
No jewel is like Rosalind. *III, ii,* 94

This is the very false gallop of verses. *III, ii,* 120

Let us make an honorable retreat, though not with
bag and baggage, yet with scrip and scrippage.
III, ii, 170

O, wonderful, wonderful, and most wonderful,
wonderful! and yet again wonderful! and after that,
out of all whooping. *III, ii,* 202

Answer me in one word. *III, ii,* 238

Do you not know I am a woman? when I think, I must
speak. *III, ii, 265*

I do desire we may be better strangers. *III, ii, 276*

Jaques: What stature is she of?
Orlando: Just as high as my heart. *III, ii, 286*

Time travels in divers paces with divers persons. I'll
tell you who Time ambles withal, who Time trots
withal, who Time gallops withal, and who he stands
still withal. *III, ii, 328*

Every one fault seeming monstrous till his fellow fault
came to match it. *III, ii, 377*

Everything about you demonstrating a careless
desolation. *III, ii, 405*

Truly, I would the gods had made thee poetical.
III, iii, 16

The wounds invisible
That love's keen arrows make. *III, v, 30*

Down on your knees,
And thank heaven, fasting, for a good man's love.
III, v, 57

Sell when you can, you are not for all markets. *III, v, 60*

I am falser than vows made in wine. *III, v, 73*

It is a melancholy of mine own, compounded of many
simples, extracted from many objects, and indeed the
sundry contemplation of my travels, which, by often
rumination, wraps me in a most humorous sadness.
IV, i, 16

I had rather have a fool to make me merry than
experience to make me sad. *IV, i, 28*

Farewell, Monsieur Traveler: look you lisp, and wear
strange suits, disable all the benefits of your own
country, be out of love with your nativity, and almost
chide God for making you that countenance you are;
or I will scarce think you have swam in a gondola.
IV, i, 35

I'll warrant him heart-whole. *IV, i, 51*

Men have died from time to time, and worms have
eaten them, but not for love. *IV, i, 110*

Forever and a day. *IV, i, 151*

Men are April when they woo, December when they
wed: maids are May when they are maids, but the sky
changes when they are wives. *IV, i, 153*

My affection hath an unknown bottom, like the bay
of Portugal. *IV, i, 219*

The horn, the horn, the lusty horn
Is not a thing to laugh to scorn. *IV, ii, 17*

Chewing the food of sweet and bitter fancy. *IV, iii, 103*

"So so," is good, very good, very excellent good: and
yet it is not; it is but so so. *V, i, 30*

The fool doth think he is wise, but the wise man
knows himself to be a fool. *V, i, 35*

No sooner met, but they looked; no sooner looked
but they loved; no sooner loved but they sighed; no
sooner sighed but they asked one another the reason;
no sooner knew the reason but they sought
the remedy. *V, ii,* 37

But, O! how bitter a thing it is to look into happiness
through another man's eyes! *V, ii,* 48

It was a lover and his lass,
With a hey, and a ho, and a hey nonino,
That o'er the green corn-field did pass,
In the spring time, the only pretty ring time,
When birds do sing, hey ding a ding, ding;
Sweet lovers love the spring. *V, iii,* 18

Here comes a pair of very strange beasts, which in all
tongues are called fools. *V, iv,* 36

An ill-favored thing, sir, but mine own. *V, iv,* 60

Rich honesty dwells like a miser, sir, in a poor house,
as your pearl in your foul oyster. *V, iv,* 62

"The retort courteous." . . . "the quip modest." . . . "the
reply churlish." . . . "the reproof valiant.". . . "the
countercheck quarrelsome." . . . "the lie circumstantial"
and "the lie direct." *V, iv, 75*

Your "if" is the only peacemaker; much virtue in "if."
V, iv, 108

He uses his folly like a stalking horse, and under the
presentation of that he shoots his wit. *V, iv, 112*

HAMLET [1600–1601]

For this relief much thanks; 'tis bitter cold,
And I am sick at heart. *Act I, sc. i, l. 8*

Not a mouse stirring. *I, i, 10*

Thou art a scholar; speak to it, Horatio. *I, i, 42*

But in the gross and scope of my opinion,
This bodes some strange eruption to our state. *I, i, 68*

Whose sore task
Does not divide the Sunday from the week. *I, i, 75*

This sweaty haste
Doth make the night joint-laborer with the day. *I, i, 77*

In the most high and palmy state of Rome,
A little ere the mightiest Julius fell,
The graves stood tenantless and the sheeted dead
Did squeak and gibber in the Roman streets. *I, i, 113*

And then it started like a guilty thing
Upon a fearful summons. *I, i, 148*

The cock, that is the trumpet to the morn. *I, i, 150*

Whether in sea or fire, in earth or air,
The extravagant and erring spirit hies
To his confine. *I, i, 153*

It faded on the crowing of the cock.
Some say that ever 'gainst that season comes
Wherein our Savior's birth is celebrated,
The bird of dawning singeth all night long;
And then, they say, no spirit can walk abroad;

The nights are wholesome; then no planets strike,
No fairy takes, nor witch hath power to charm,
So hallow'd and so gracious is the time. *I, i, 157*

But, look, the morn in russet mantle clad,
Walks o'er the dew of yon high eastern hill. *I, i, 166*

The memory be green. *I, ii, 2*

With one auspicious and one dropping eye,
With mirth in funeral and with dirge in marriage,
In equal scale weighing delight and dole. *I, ii, 11*

So much for him. *I, ii, 25*

A little more than kin, and less than kind. *I, ii, 65*

Thou know'st 'tis common; all that live must die,
Passing through nature to eternity. *I, ii, 72*

Seems, madam! Nay, it is; I know not "seems."
'Tis not alone my inky cloak, good mother,
Nor customary suits of solemn black. *I, ii, 76*

But I have that within which passeth show;
These but the trappings and the suits of woe.   *I, ii, 85*

To persever
In obstinate condolement is a course
Of impious stubbornness; 'tis unmanly grief:
It shows a will most incorrect to heaven,
A heart unfortified, a mind impatient.   *I, ii, 92*

O! that this too too solid flesh would melt,
Thaw and resolve itself into a dew;
Or that the Everlasting had not fix'd
His canon 'gainst self-slaughter! O God! O God!
How weary, stale, flat, and unprofitable
Seem to me all the uses of this world.   *I, ii, 129*

Things rank and gross in nature
Possess it merely. That it should come to this!   *I, ii, 136*

So excellent a king; that was, to this,
Hyperion to a satyr; so loving to my mother
That he might not beteem the winds of heaven
Visit her face too roughly.   *I, ii, 139*

Why, she would hang on him,
As if increase of appetite had grown
    By what it fed on. *I, ii, 143*

Frailty, thy name is woman! *I, ii, 146*

Like Niobe, all tears. *I, ii, 149*

A beast, that wants discourse of reason. *I, ii, 150*

It is not nor it cannot come to good. *I, ii, 158*

A truant disposition. *I, ii, 169*

Thrift, thrift, Horatio! the funeral bak'd meats
Did coldly furnish forth the marriage tables.
Would I had met my dearest foe in heaven
    Ere I had ever seen that day. *I, ii, 180*

In my mind's eye, Horatio. *I, ii, 185*

He was a man, take him for all in all,
I shall not look upon his like again. *I, ii, 187*

Season your admiration for a while. *I, ii, 192*

In the dead vast and middle of the night. *I, ii, 198*

Armed at points exactly, cap-a-pe. *I, ii, 200*

Distill'd
Almost to jelly with the act of fear. *I, ii, 204*

A countenance more in sorrow than in anger. *I, ii, 231*

Hamlet: His beard was grizzled, no?
Horatio: It was, as I have seen it in his life,
A sable silver'd. *I, ii, 239*

Give it an understanding, but no tongue. *I, ii, 249*

All is not well;
I doubt some foul play. *I, ii, 254*

Foul deeds will rise,
Though all the earth o'erwhelm them, to men's eyes.
I, ii, 256

The chariest maid is prodigal enough
If she unmask her beauty to the moon;
Virtue itself 'scapes not calumnious strokes;
The canker galls the infants of the spring
Too oft before their buttons be disclos'd,
And in the morn and liquid dew of youth
Contagious blastments are most imminent. *I, iii,* 36

Do not, as some ungracious pastors do,
Show me the steep and thorny way to heaven,
Whiles, like a puff'd and reckless libertine,
Himself the primrose path of dalliance treads,
And recks not his own rede. *I, iii,* 47

Give thy thoughts no tongue. *I, iii,* 59

Be thou familiar, but by no means vulgar;
Those friends thou hast, and their adoption tried,
Grapple them to thy soul with hoops of steel. *I, iii,* 61

Beware
Of entrance to a quarrel, but, being in,
Bear 't that th' opposed may beware of thee.
Give every man thy ear, but few thy voice;
Take each man's censure, but reserve thy judgment.
Costly thy habit as thy purse can buy,
But not express'd in fancy; rich, not gaudy;
For the apparel oft proclaims the man. *I, iii,* 65

Neither a borrower, nor a lender be;
For loan oft loses both itself and friend,
And borrowing dulls the edge of husbandry.
This above all: to thine own self be true,
And it must follow, as the night the day,
Thou canst not then be false to any man.   *I, iii, 75*

'Tis in my memory lock'd,
And you yourself shall keep the key of it.   *I, iii, 85*

You speak like a green girl,
Unsifted in such perilous circumstance.   *I, iii, 101*

Springes to catch woodcocks.   *I, iii, 115*

When the blood burns, how prodigal the soul
Lends the tongue vows.   *I, iii, 116*

Be somewhat scanter of your maiden presence.   *I, iii, 121*

The air bites shrewdly.   *I, iv, 1*

But to my mind, — though I am native here
And to the manner born — it is a custom
More honor'd in the breach than the observance.

I, iv, 14

Angels and ministers of grace defend us! *I, iv, 39*

Be thy intents wicked or charitable,
Thou com'st in such a questionable shape
That I will speak to thee. *I, iv, 42*

What may this mean,
That thou, dead corse, again in complete steel
Revisit'st thus the glimpses of the moon,
Making night hideous; and we fools of nature
So horridly to shake our disposition
With thoughts beyond the reaches of our souls? *I, iv, 51*

I do not set my life at a pin's fee. *I, iv, 65*

The dreadful summit of the cliff
That beetles o'er his base into the sea. *I, iv, 70*

My fate cries out,
And makes each petty artery in this body
As hardy as the Nemean lion's nerve. *I, iv, 81*

Unhand me, gentlemen,
By heaven! I'll make a ghost of him that lets me. *I, iv, 84*

Something is rotten in the state of Denmark. *I, iv, 90*

I could a tale unfold whose lightest word
Would harrow up thy soul, freeze thy young blood,
Make thy two eyes, like stars, start from their spheres,
Thy knotted and combined locks to part,
And each particular hair to stand an end,
Like quills upon the fretful porpentine. *I, v, 15*

Murder most foul, as in the best it is. *I, v, 27*

And duller shouldst thou be than the fat weed
That rots itself in ease on Lethe wharf. *I, v, 32*

O my prophetic soul!
My uncle! *I, v, 40*

O Hamlet! what a falling-off was there. *I, v, 47*

But virtue, as it never will be mov'd,
Though lewdness court it in a shape of heaven,
So lust, though to a radiant angel link'd,
Will sate itself in a celestial bed,
And prey on garbage. *I, v, 53*

In the porches of mine ears. *I, v, 63*

Cut off even in the blossoms of my sin,
Unhousel'd, disappointed, unanel'd,
No reckoning made, but sent to my account
With all my imperfections on my head. *I, v, 76*

Leave her to heaven,
And to those thorns that in her bosom lodge,
To prick and sting her. *I, v, 86*

The glowworm shows the matin to be near,
And 'gins to pale his uneffectual fire. *I, v, 89*

While memory holds a seat
In this distracted globe. Remember thee!
Yea, from the table of my memory
I'll wipe away all trivial fond records. *I, v, 96*

Within the book and volume of my brain. *I, v, 103*

O villain, villain, smiling, damned villain!
My tables — meet it is I set it down,
That one may smile, and smile, and be a villain;
At least I'm sure it may be so in Denmark. *I, v, 106*

There's ne'er a villain dwelling in all Denmark,
But he's an arrant knave. *I, v, 123*

There are more things in heaven and earth, Horatio,
Than are dreamt of in your philosophy. *I, v, 166*

To put an antic disposition on. *I, v, 172*

Rest, rest, perturbed spirit! *I, v, 182*

The time is out of joint; O cursed spite,
That ever I was born to set it right! *I, v, 188*

Your bait of falsehood takes this carp of truth;
And thus do we of wisdom and of reach,
With windlasses and with assays of bias,
By indirections find directions out. *II, i, 63*

Ungarter'd, and down-gyved to his ankle. *II, i, 80*

This is the very ecstasy of love. *II, i, 102*

Brevity is the soul of wit. *II, ii, 90*

More matter, with less art. *II, ii, 95*

That he is mad, 'tis true; 'tis true 'tis pity;
And pity 'tis 'tis true. *II, ii, 97*

Find out the cause of this effect,
Or rather say, the cause of this defect,
For this effect defective comes by cause. *II, ii, 101*

Doubt thou the stars are fire;
Doubt that the sun doth move;
Doubt truth to be a liar;
But never doubt I love. *II, ii, 115*

Polonius: Do you know me, my lord?
Hamlet: Excellent well; you are a fishmonger. *II, ii, 173*

To be honest, as this world goes, is to be one man
picked out of ten thousand. *II, ii, 179*

Hamlet: For if the sun breed maggots in a dead dog,
being a god kissing carrion, — Have you a daughter?
Polonius: I have, my lord.
Hamlet: Let her not walk i' the sun. *II, ii, 183*

Still harping on my daughter. *II, ii, 190*

Polonius: What do you read, my lord?
Hamlet: Words, words, words. *II, ii, 195*

They have a plentiful lack of wit. *II, ii, 204*

Though this be madness, yet there is method in 't.
II, ii, 211

These tedious old fools! *II, ii, 227*

The indifferent children of the earth. *II, ii, 235*

Happy in that we are not over happy. *II, ii, 236*

There is nothing either good or bad, but thinking
makes it so. *II, ii, 259*

O God! I could be bounded in a nutshell, and count
myself a king of infinite space, were it not that I have
bad dreams. *II, ii, 263*

Beggar that I am, I am even poor in thanks. *II, ii, 286*

This goodly frame, the earth, seems to me a sterile
promontory; this most excellent canopy, the air, look
you, this brave o'erhanging firmament, this majestical
roof fretted with golden fire, why, it appears no other
thing to me but a foul and pestilent congregation of
vapors. What a piece of work is a man! How noble in
reason! how infinite in faculty! in form, in moving,
how express and admirable! in action how like an
angel! in apprehension how like a god! *II, ii,* 317

And yet, to me, what is this quintessence of dust? man
delights not me; no, nor woman neither. *II, ii,* 328

There is something in this more than natural, if
philosophy could find it out. *II, ii,* 392

I am but mad north-northwest: when the wind is
southerly I know a hawk from a handsaw. *II, ii,* 405

They say an old man is twice a child. *II, ii,* 413

One fair daughter and no more,
The which he loved passing well. *II, ii,* 435

Come, give us a taste of your quality. *II, ii,* 460

The play, I remember, pleased not the million; 'twas
caviare to the general. *II, ii, 465*

They are the abstracts and brief chronicles of the
time: after your death you were better have a bad
epitaph than their ill report while you live. *II, ii, 555*

Use every man after his desert, and who should 'scape
whipping? *II, ii, 561*

O! what a rogue and peasant slave am I. *II, ii, 584*

What's Hecuba to him or he to Hecuba,
That he should weep for her? *II, ii, 593*

Who calls me villain? breaks my pate across?
Plucks off my beard and blows it in my face? *II, ii, 607*

But I am pigeon-liver'd, and lack gall
To make oppression bitter. *II, ii, 613*

The play's the thing
Wherein I'll catch the conscience of the king. *II, ii, 641*

With devotion's visage
And pious action we do sugar o'er
The devil himself. *III, i, 47*

To be, or not to be: that is the question:
Whether 'tis nobler in the mind to suffer
The slings and arrows of outrageous fortune,
Or to take arms against a sea of troubles,
And by opposing end them? To die: to sleep;
No more; and, by a sleep to say we end
The heartache and the thousand natural shocks
That flesh is heir to, 'tis a consummation
Devoutly to be wish'd. To die, to sleep;
To sleep: perchance to dream: ay, there's the rub;
For in that sleep of death what dreams may come
When we have shuffled off this mortal coil,
Must give us pause. There's the respect
That makes calamity of so long life;
For who would bear the whips and scorns of time,
The oppressor's wrong, the proud man's contumely,
The pangs of dispriz'd love, the law's delay,
The insolence of office, and the spurns
That patient merit of the unworthy takes,
When he himself might his quietus make
With a bare bodkin? who would fardels bear,
To grunt and sweat under a weary life,
But that the dread of something after death,
The undiscover'd country from whose bourn

No traveler returns, puzzles the will,
And makes us rather bear those ills we have
Than fly to others that we know not of?
Thus conscience does make cowards of us all;
And thus the native hue of resolution
Is sicklied o'er with the pale cast of thought,
And enterprises of great pith and moment
With this regard their currents turn awry,
And lose the name of action. *III, i, 56*

Nymph, in thy orisons
Be all my sins remember'd. *III, i, 89*

To the noble mind
Rich gifts wax poor when givers prove
unkind. *III, i, 100*

Get thee to a nunnery. *III, i, 124*

What should such fellows as I do crawling between
heaven and earth? We are arrant knaves, all. *III, i, 128*

Be thou as chaste as ice, as pure as snow, thou shalt
not escape calumny. *III, i, 142*

I have heard of your paintings too, well enough; God
has given you one face, and you make yourselves
another. *III, i, 150*

O! what a noble mind is here o'erthrown:
The courtier's, soldier's, scholar's, eye, tongue, sword.
III, i, 159

The glass of fashion and the mould of form,
The observ'd of all observers! *III, i, 162*

Now see that noble and most sovereign reason,
Like sweet bells jangled, out of tune and harsh.
III, i, 166

O! woe is me,
To have seen what I have seen, see what I see! *III, i, 169*

Speak the speech, I pray you, as I pronounced it to
you, trippingly on the tongue; but if you mouth it, as
many of your players do, I had as lief the town-crier
spoke my lines. Nor do not saw the air too much with
your hand, thus; but use all gently: for in the very
torrent, tempest, and — as I may say — whirlwind of
passion, you must acquire and beget a temperance,
that may give it smoothness. O! it offends me to the

soul to hear a robustious periwig-pated fellow tear a
passion to tatters, to very rags, to split the ears of the
groundlings, who for the most part are capable of
nothing but inexplicable dumb-shows and noise: I
would have such a fellow whipped for o'erdoing
Termagant; it out-herods Herod. *III, ii, 1*

Suit the action to the word, the word to the action;
with this special observance, that you o'erstep not the
modesty of nature. *III, ii,* 20

To hold, as 'twere, the mirror up to nature; to show
virtue her own feature, scorn her own image, and the
very age and body of the time his form and pressure.
III, ii, 25

I have thought some of nature's journeymen had made
men and not made them well, they imitated humanity
so abominably. *III, ii,* 38

No; let the candied tongue lick absurd pomp,
And crook the pregnant hinges of the knee
Where thrift may follow fawning. *III, ii,* 65

A man that fortune's buffets and rewards
Hast ta'en with equal thanks. *III, ii,* 72

They are not a pipe for fortune's finger
To sound what stop she please. Give me that man
That is not passion's slave, and I will wear him
In my heart's core, ay, in my heart of heart,
As I do thee. Something too much of this. *III, ii, 75*

My imaginations are as foul
As Vulcan's stithy. *III, ii, 88*

The chameleon's dish: I eat the air, promise-crammed;
you cannot feed capons so. *III, ii, 98*

Nay, then, let the devil wear black, for I'll have a suit
of sables. *III, ii, 138*

There's hope a great man's memory may outlive his
life half a year. *III, ii, 141*

Marry, this is miching mallecho; it means mischief.
III, ii, 148

Ophelia: 'Tis brief, my lord.
Hamlet: As woman's love. *III, ii, 165*

Where love is great, the littlest doubts are fear;
When little fears grow great, great love grows there.
III, ii, 183

Wormwood, wormwood. *III, ii, 193*

The lady doth protest too much, methinks. *III, ii, 242*

Let the galled jade wince, our withers are unwrung.
III, ii, 256

Why, let the stricken deer go weep,
The hart ungalled play;
For some must watch, while some must sleep:
So runs the world away. *III, ii, 287*

You would pluck out the heart of my mystery. *III, ii, 389*

Do you think I am easier to be played on than a pipe?
III, ii, 393

Hamlet: Do you see yonder cloud that's almost in shape
of a camel?
Polonius: By the mass, and 'tis like a camel, indeed.
Hamlet: Methinks it is like a weasel.
Polonius: It is backed like a weasel.
Hamlet: Or like a whale?
Polonius: Very like a whale. *III, ii,* 400

They fool me to the top of my bent. *III, ii,* 408

By and by is easily said. *III, ii,* 411

'Tis now the very witching time of night,
When churchyards yawn and hell itself breathes out
Contagion to this world. *III, ii,* 413

I will speak daggers to her, but use none. *III, ii,* 421

O! my offense is rank, it smells to heaven;
It hath the primal eldest curse upon 't;
A brother's murder! *III, iii,* 36

Now might I do it pat, now he is praying;
And now I'll do 't: and so he goes to heaven;
And so I am reveng'd. *III, iii,* 73

With all his crimes broad blown, as flush as May.
III, iii, 81

My words fly up, my thoughts remain below:
Words without thoughts never to heaven go. *III, iii,* 97

How now! a rat? Dead, for a ducat, dead! *III, iv,* 23

False as dicers' oaths. *III, iv,* 45

A rhapsody of words. *III, iv,* 48

See, what a grace was seated on this brow;
Hyperion's curls, the front of Jove himself,
An eye like Mars, to threaten and command,
A station like the herald Mercury
New-lighted on a heaven-kissing hill,
A combination and a form indeed,
Where every god did seem to set his seal,
To give the world assurance of a man. *III, iv,* 55

At your age
The heyday in the blood is tame, it's humble. *III, iv,* 68

O shame! where is thy blush? Rebellious hell,
If thou canst mutine in a matron's bones,
To flaming youth let virtue be as wax,
And melt in her own fire: proclaim no shame
When the compulsive ardor gives the charge,
Since frost itself as actively doth burn,
And reason panders will. *III, iv,* 82

A king of shreds and patches. *III, iv,* 102

Lay not that flattering unction to your soul. *III, iv,* 145

Confess yourself to heaven;
Repent what's past; avoid what is to come. *III, iv,* 149

For in the fatness of these pursy times
Virtue itself of vice must pardon beg. *III, iv,* 153

Assume a virtue, if you have it not. *III, iv,* 160

Refrain tonight;
And that shall lend a kind of easiness
To the next abstinence: the next more easy;
For use almost can change the stamp of nature. *III, iv,* 165

I must be cruel only to be kind. *III, iv,* 178

For 'tis the sport to have the enginer
Hoist with his own petar. *III, iv, 206*

Diseases desperate grown
By desperate appliance are relieved,
Or not at all. *IV, iii, 9*

A man may fish with the worm that hath eat of a king,
and eat of the fish that hath fed of that worm. *IV, iii, 29*

We go to gain a little patch of ground
That hath in it no profit but the name. *IV, iv, 18*

How all occasions do inform against me,
And spur my dull revenge! What is a man,
If his chief good and market of his time
Be but to sleep and feed? a beast, no more.
Sure he that made us with such large discourse,
Looking before and after, gave us not
That capability and godlike reason
To fust in us unus'd. *IV, iv, 32*

Some craven scruple
Of thinking too precisely on the event. *IV, iv, 40*

Rightly to be great
Is not to stir without great argument,
But greatly to find quarrel in a straw
When honor's at the stake. *IV, iv, 53*

So full of artless jealousy is guilt,
It spills itself in fearing to be spilt. *IV, v, 19*

How should I your true love know
From another one?
By his cockle hat and staff,
And his sandal shoon. *IV, v, 23*

He is dead and gone, lady,
He is dead and gone;
At his head a grass-green turf
At his heels a stone. *IV, v, 29*

We know what we are, but know not what we may be.
IV, v, 43

Come, my coach! Good night, ladies; good night,
sweet ladies; good night, good night. *IV, v, 72*

When sorrows come, they come not single spies,
But in battalions. *IV, v, 78*

We have done but greenly,
In hugger-mugger to inter him. *IV, v,* 84

There's such divinity doth hedge a king,
That treason can but peep to what it would. *IV, v,* 123

There's rosemary, that's for remembrance . . . and
there is pansies, that's for thoughts. *IV, v,* 174

O! you must wear your rue with a difference. There's a
daisy; I would give you some violets, but they
withered all when my father died. *IV, v,* 181

A very riband in the cap of youth. *IV, vii,* 77

Nature her custom holds,
Let shame say what it will. *IV, vii,* 188

There is no ancient gentlemen but gardeners, ditchers,
and grave-makers; they hold up Adam's profession.
V, i, 32

Cudgel thy brains no more about it. *V, i,* 61

Has this fellow no feeling of his business, that he sings
at grave-making? *V, i,* 71

Custom hath made it in him a property of easiness.
V, i, 73

A politician . . . one that would circumvent God.
V, i, 84

Why may not that be the skull of a lawyer? Where be
his quiddities now, his quillets, his cases, his tenures,
and his tricks? *V, i,* 104

One that was a woman, sir; but, rest her soul, she's
dead. *V, i,* 145

How absolute the knave is! we must speak by the
card, or equivocation will undo us. *V, i,* 147

The age is grown so picked that the toe of the peasant
comes so near the heel of the courtier, he galls
his kibe. *V, i,* 150

Alas! poor Yorick. I knew him, Horatio; a fellow of
infinite jest, of most excellent fancy; he hath borne me
on his back a thousand times; and now, how abhorred
    in my imagination it is! my gorge rises at it. Here
hung those lips that I have kissed I know not how oft.
Where be your gibes now? your gambols? your songs?
  your flashes of merriment, that were wont to set the
    table on a roar? Not one now, to mock your own
grinning? quite chapfallen? Now get you to my lady's
chamber, and tell her, let her paint an inch thick, to
    this favor she must come; make her laugh at that.
V, i, 201

To what base uses we may return, Horatio! Why may
not imagination trace the noble dust of Alexander, till
    he find it stopping a bung-hole? *V, i, 222*

Imperious Caesar, dead and turn'd to clay,
Might stop a hole to keep the wind away. *V, i, 235*

Lay her i' the earth;
And from her fair and unpolluted flesh
May violets spring! *V, i, 260*

A ministering angel shall my sister be. *V, i, 263*

Sweets to the sweet: farewell! *V, i, 265*

I thought thy bride-bed to have deck'd, sweet maid,
    And not have strew'd thy grave. *V, i, 267*

Though I am not splenetive and rash
Yet have I in me something dangerous. *V, i, 283*

I lov'd Ophelia: forty thousand brothers
Could not, with all their quantity of love,
    Make up my sum. *V, i, 291*

Nay, an thou'lt mouth,
I'll rant as well as thou. *V, i, 305*

Let Hercules himself do what he may,
The cat will mew and dog will have his day. *V, i, 313*

There's a divinity that shapes our ends,
    Rough-hew them how we will. *V, ii, 10*

I once did hold it, as our statists do,
    A baseness to write fair. *V, ii, 33*

It did me yeoman's service. *V, ii, 36*

Not a whit, we defy augury; there's a special
providence in the fall of a sparrow. If it be now, 'tis not
to come; if it be not to come, it will be now; if it be
not now, yet it will come: the readiness is all. *V, ii, 232*

A hit, a very palpable hit. *V, ii, 295*

This fell sergeant, death,
Is strict in his arrest. *V, ii, 350*

Report me and my cause aright. *V, ii, 353*

I am more an antique Roman than a Dane. *V, ii, 355*

O God! Horatio, what a wounded name,
Things standing thus unknown, shall live behind me.
If thou didst ever hold me in thy heart,
Absent thee from felicity awhile,
And in this harsh world draw thy breath in pain,
To tell my story. *V, ii, 358*

The rest is silence. *V, ii, 372*

Now cracks a noble heart. Good night, sweet prince,
And flights of angels sing thee to thy rest! *V, ii, 373*

O proud death!
What feast is toward in thine eternal cell? *V, ii, 378*

THE PHOENIX AND THE TURTLE [1601]

Property was thus appall'd,
That the self was not the same;
Single nature's double name
Neither two nor one was call'd. *l. 37*

Reason, in itself confounded,
Saw division grow together. *l. 41*

TROILUS AND CRESSIDA [1601–1602]

The chance of war. *Prologue, l. 31*

I have had my labor for my travail. *Act I, sc. i, l. 73*

Women are angels, wooing:
Things won are done; joy's soul lies in the doing.
I, ii, 310

Men prize the thing ungain'd more than it is. *I, ii, 313*

The sea being smooth,
How many shallow bauble boats dare sail
Upon her patient breast. *I, iii, 34*

The heavens themselves, the planets, and this center
Observe degree, priority, and place,
Insisture, course, proportion, season, form,
Office, and custom, in all line of order. *I, iii, 85*

O! when degree is shaked,
Which is the ladder to all high designs,
The enterprise is sick. *I, iii, 101*

Take but degree away, untune that string,
And, hark! what discord follows; each thing meets
In mere oppugnancy: the bounded waters
Should lift their bosoms higher than the shores,
And make a sop of all this solid globe. *I, iii, 109*

Then everything includes itself in power,
Power into will, will into appetite;
And appetite, a universal wolf,
So doubly seconded with will and power,
Must make perforce a universal prey,
And last eat up himself. *I, iii, 119*

Like a strutting player, whose conceit
Lies in his hamstring, and doth think it rich
To hear the wooden dialogue and sound
'Twixt his stretch'd footing and the scaffoldage.

I, iii, 153

And in such indexes, although small pricks
To their subsequent volumes, there is seen
The baby figure of the giant mass
Of things to come. *I, iii, 343*

Who wears his wit in his belly, and his guts
in his head. *II, i, 78*

Modest doubt is call'd
The beacon of the wise, the tent that searches
To the bottom of the worst. *II, ii, 15*

'Tis mad idolatry
To make the service greater than the god. *II, ii, 56*

He that is proud eats up himself; pride is his own glass, his
own trumpet, his own chronicle. *II, iii, 165*

I am giddy, expectation whirls me round.
The imaginary relish is so sweet
That it enchants my sense. *III, ii, 17*

Words pay no debts. *III, ii, 56*

To fear the worst oft cures the worse. *III, ii, 77*

All lovers swear more performance than they are able,
and yet reserve an ability that they never perform;
vowing more than the perfection of ten and
discharging less than the tenth part of one. *III, ii, 89*

For to be wise, and love,
Exceeds man's might; that dwells with gods above.
III, ii, 163

If I be false, or swerve a hair from truth,
When time is old and hath forgot itself,
When waterdrops have worn the stones of Troy,
And blind oblivion swallow'd cities up.
And mighty states characterless are grated
To dusty nothing, yet let memory,
From false to false, among false maids in love
Upbraid my falsehood! when they have said "as false
As air, as water, wind, or sandy earth,

As fox to lamb, as wolf to heifer's calf,
Pard to the hind, or stepdame to her son";
Yea, let them say, to stick the heart of falsehood,
"As false as Cressid."   *III, ii, 191*

Time hath, my lord, a wallet at his back,
Wherein he puts alms for oblivion.   *III, iii, 145*

Perseverance, dear my lord,
Keeps honor bright: to have done, is to hang
Quite out of fashion, like a rusty mail
In monumental mockery.   *III, iii, 150*

For honor travels in a strait so narrow
Where one but goes abreast.   *III, iii, 154*

Time is like a fashionable host,
That slightly shakes his parting guest by the hand,
And with his arms outstretch'd, as he would fly,
Grasps in the comer: welcome ever smiles,
And farewell goes out sighing.   *III, iii, 168*

Beauty, wit,
High birth, vigor of bone, desert in service,
Love, friendship, charity, are subjects all
To envious and calumniating time.
One touch of nature makes the whole world kin.

III, iii, 171

And give to dust that is a little gilt
More laud than gilt o'er-dusted. *III, iii, 178*

My mind is troubled, like a fountain stirr'd;
And I myself see not the bottom of it. *III, iii, 314*

You do as chapmen do,
Dispraise the thing that you desire to buy. *IV, i, 75*

As many farewells as be stars in heaven. *IV, iv, 44*

And sometimes we are devils to ourselves
When we will tempt the frailty of our powers,
Presuming on their changeful potency. *IV, iv, 95*

The kiss you take is better than you give. *IV, v, 38*

Fie, fie upon her!
There's language in her eye, her cheek, her lip,
Nay, her foot speaks; her wanton spirits look out
At every joint and motive of her body. *IV, v, 54*

What's past and what's to come is strew'd with husks
And formless ruin of oblivion. *IV, v, 165*

The end crowns all,
And that old common arbitrator, Time,
Will one day end it. *IV, v, 223*

Words, words, mere words, no matter from the heart.
V, iii, 109

Hector is dead; there is no more to say. *V, x, 22*

O world! world! world! thus is the poor agent
despised. *V, x, 36*

TWELFTH-NIGHT [1601–1602]

If music be the food of love, play on;
Give me excess of it, that, surfeiting,
The appetite may sicken, and so die.
That strain again! it had a dying fall:
O! it came o'er my ear like the sweet sound
That breathes upon a bank of violets,
Stealing and giving odor!   *Act I, sc. i, l. 1*

O spirit of love! how quick and fresh art thou,
That, notwithstanding thy capacity
Receiveth as the sea, nought enters there,
Of what validity and pitch soe'er,
But falls into abatement and low price,
Even in a minute: so full of shapes is fancy,
That it alone is high fantastical.   *I, i, 9*

When my tongue blabs, then let mine eyes not see.
I, ii, 61

I am sure care's an enemy to life.   *I, iii, 2*

Let them hang themselves in their own straps.   *I, iii, 13*

I am a great eater of beef, and I believe that does harm
to my wit. *I, iii, 92*

Wherefore are these things hid? *I, iii, 135*

Is it a world to hide virtues in? *I, iii, 142*

God give them wisdom that have it; and those that
are fools, let them use their talents. *I, v, 14*

One draught above heat makes him a fool, the second
mads him, and a third drowns him. *I, v, 139*

'Tis beauty truly blent, whose red and white
Nature's own sweet and cunning hand laid on:
Lady, you are the cruel'st she alive,
If you will lead these graces to the grave
And leave the world no copy. *I, v, 259*

Make me a willow cabin at your gate,
And call upon my soul within the house. *I, v, 289*

Holla your name to the reverberate hills,
And make the babbling gossip of the air
Cry out, "Olivia!" *I, v, 293*

Farewell, fair cruelty. *I, v, 309*

O mistress mine! where are you roaming? *II, iii, 42*

Journeys end in lovers meeting,
Every wise man's son doth know. *II, iii, 46*

What is love? 'tis not hereafter;
Present mirth hath present laughter.
What's to come is still unsure:
In delay there lies no plenty;
Then come kiss me, sweet and twenty,
Youth's a stuff will not endure. *II, iii, 50*

He does it with a better grace, but I do it more
natural. *II, iii, 91*

Is there no respect of place, persons, nor time, in you?
II, iii, 100

Sir Toby: Dost thou think, because thou art virtuous,
there shall be no more cakes and ale?
Clown: Yes, by Saint Anne; and ginger shall be hot i'
the mouth too. *II, iii, 124*

The devil a puritan that he is, or anything constantly
but a time-pleaser; an affectioned ass. *II, iii, 161*

My purpose is, indeed, a horse of that color. *II, iii, 184*

These most brisk and giddy-paced times. *II, iv, 6*

If ever thou shalt love,
In the sweet pangs of it remember me;
For such as I am all true lovers are:
Unstaid and skittish in all motions else
Save in the constant image of the creature
That is belov'd. *II, iv, 15*

Let still the woman take
An elder than herself, so wears she to him,
So sways she level in her husband's heart:
For, boy, however we do praise ourselves,
Our fancies are more giddy and unfirm,
More longing, wavering, sooner lost and worn,
Than women's are. *II, iv, 29*

Then, let thy love be younger than thyself,
Or thy affection cannot hold the bent;
For women are as roses, whose fair flower
Being once display'd, doth fall that very hour. *II, iv, 36*

The spinsters and the knitters in the sun,
And the free maids that weave their thread with bones,
Do use to chant it: it is silly sooth,
And dallies with the innocence of love,
Like the old age. *II, iv, 44*

Come away, come away, death,
And in sad cypress let me be laid;
Fly away, fly away, breath;
I am slain by a fair cruel maid. *II, iv, 51*

Duke: And what's her history?
Viola: A blank, my lord. She never told her love,
But let concealment, like a worm i' the bud,
Feed on her damask cheek: she pin'd in thought,
And with a green and yellow melancholy,
She sat like Patience on a monument,
Smiling at grief. *II, iv, 112*

I am all the daughters of my father's house,
And all the brothers too. *II, iv, 122*

Here comes the trout that must be caught with
tickling. *II, v, 25*

I may command where I adore. *II, v, 116*

Be not afraid of greatness: some are born great, some achieve greatness, and some have greatness thrust upon them. *II, v, 159*

Remember who commended thy yellow stockings, and wished to see thee ever cross-gartered. *II, v, 168*

Foolery, sir, does walk about the orb like the sun; it shines everywhere. *III, i, 44*

This fellow's wise enough to play the fool, And to do that well craves a kind of wit. *III, i, 68*

Music from the spheres. *III, i, 122*

How apt the poor are to be proud. *III, i, 141*

Then westward-ho! *III, i, 148*

O! what a deal of scorn looks beautiful In the contempt and anger of his lip. *III, i, 159*

Love sought is good, but giv'n unsought is better.
III, i, 170

You will hang like an icicle on a Dutchman's beard.
III, ii, 30

Let there be gall enough in thy ink.   *III, ii,* 54

Laugh yourselves into stitches.   *III, ii,* 75

I think we do know the sweet Roman hand.   *III, iv,* 31

This is very midsummer madness.   *III, iv,* 62

More matter for a May morning.   *III, iv,* 158

He's a very devil.   *III, iv,* 304

Out of my lean and low ability
I'll lend you something.   *III, iv,* 380

I hate ingratitude more in a man
Than lying, vainness, babbling drunkenness,
Or any taint of vice whose strong corruption
Inhabits our frail blood. *III, iv, 390*

As the old hermit of Prague, that never saw pen and
ink, very wittily said to a niece of King Gorboduc,
"That, that is, is." *IV, ii, 14*

I say there is no darkness but ignorance, in which
thou art more puzzled than the Egyptians in their fog.
IV, ii, 47

Thus the whirligig of time brings in
his revenges. *V, i, 388*

When that I was and a little tiny boy,
With hey, ho, the wind and the rain;
A foolish thing was but a toy,
For the rain it raineth every day. *V, i, 404*

ALL'S WELL THAT ENDS WELL [1602–1604]

Love all, trust a few,
Do wrong to none: be able for thine enemy
Rather in power than use, and keep thy friend
Under thy own life's key: be check'd for silence,
But never tax'd for speech. *Act I, sc. i, l. 74*

It were all one
That I should love a bright particular star
And think to wed it, he is so above me. *I, i, 97*

The hind that would be mated by the lion
Must die for love. *I, i, 103*

My friends were poor, but honest. *I, iii, 203*

Oft expectation fails, and most oft there
Where most it promises. *II, i, 145*

They say miracles are past. *II, iii, 1*

A young man married is a man that's marr'd. *II, iii, 315*

The web of our life is of a mingled yarn, good and ill
together. *IV, iii, 83*

There's place and means for every man alive. *IV, iii, 379*

All's well that ends well: still the fine's the crown;
Whate'er the course, the end is the renown. *IV, iv, 35*

I am a man whom Fortune hath cruelly scratched.
V, ii, 28

Praising what is lost
Makes the remembrance dear. *V, iii, 19*

The inaudible and noiseless foot of time. *V, iii, 41*

Love that comes too late,
Like a remorseful pardon slowly carried. *V, iii, 57*

All impediments in fancy's course
Are motives of more fancy. *V, iii, 216*

MEASURE FOR MEASURE [1604]

Good counselors lack no clients.   *Act I, sc. ii, l. 115*

And liberty plucks justice by the nose.   *I, iii, 29*

I hold you as a thing ensky'd and sainted.   *I, iv, 34*

A man whose blood
Is very snow-broth; one who never feels
The wanton stings and motions of the sense.   *I, iv, 57*

Our doubts are traitors,
And make us lose the good we oft might win,
By fearing to attempt.   *I, iv, 78*

We must not make a scarecrow of the law,
Setting it up to fear the birds of prey,
And let it keep one shape, till custom make it
Their perch and not their terror.   *II, i, 1*

The jury, passing on the prisoner's life,
May in the sworn twelve have a thief or two
Guiltier than him they try.   *II, i, 19*

Some rise by sin, and some by virtue fall. *II, i, 38*

Great with child, and longing . . . for stewed prunes.
II, i, 94

This will last out a night in Russia,
When nights are longest there. *II, i, 144*

His face is the worst thing about him. *II, i, 167*

Condemn the fault, and not the actor of it? *II, ii, 37*

No ceremony that to great ones 'longs,
Not the king's crown, nor the deputed sword,
The marshal's truncheon, nor the judge's robe,
Become them with one half so good a grace
As mercy does. *II, ii, 59*

The law hath not been dead, though it hath slept.
II, ii, 90

O! it is excellent
To have a giant's strength, but it is tyrannous
To use it like a giant. *II, ii, 107*

But man, proud man,
Drest in a little brief authority,
Most ignorant of what he's most assur'd,
His glassy essence, like an angry ape,
Plays such fantastic tricks before high heaven
As make the angels weep.　*II, ii, 117*

That in the captain's but a choleric word,
Which in the soldier is flat blasphemy.　*II, ii, 130*

It oft falls out,
To have what we would have, we speak not what we
mean.　*II, iv, 118*

The miserable have no other medicine
But only hope.　*III, i, 2*

Be absolute for death.　*III, i, 5*

A breath thou art,
Servile to all the skyey influences.　*III, i, 8*

Thou hast nor youth nor age;
But, as it were, an after-dinner's sleep,
Dreaming on both; for all thy blessed youth
Becomes as aged, and doth beg the alms
Of palsied eld; and when thou art old and rich,
Thou hast neither heat, affection, limb, nor beauty,
To make thy riches pleasant. *III, i,* 32

The sense of death is most in apprehension,
And the poor beetle, that we tread upon,
In corporal sufferance finds a pang as great
As when a giant dies. *III, i,* 76

If I must die,
I will encounter darkness as a bride,
And hug it in my arms. *III, i,* 81

The cunning livery of hell. *III, i,* 93

Ay, but to die, and go we know not where;
To lie in cold obstruction and to rot;
This sensible warm motion to become
A kneaded clod; and the delighted spirit
To bathe in fiery floods, or to reside
In thrilling region of thick-ribbed ice;
To be imprison'd in the viewless winds,
And blown with restless violence round about
The pendant world. *III, i,* 116

The weariest and most loathed worldly life
That age, ache, penury, and imprisonment
Can lay on nature is a paradise
To what we fear of death. *III, i,* 127

The hand that hath made you fair hath made you
good. *III, i,* 182

Virtue is bold, and goodness never fearful. *III, i,* 214

There, at the moated grange, resides this dejected
Mariana. *III, i,* 279

This news is old enough, yet it is every day's news.
III, ii, 249

He, who the sword of heaven will bear
Should be as holy as severe. *III, ii,* 283

O, what may man within him hide,
Though angel on the outward side! *III, ii,* 293

Take, O take those lips away,
That so sweetly were forsworn;
And those eyes, the break of day,
Lights that do mislead the morn:
But my kisses bring again, bring again,
Seals of love, but seal'd in vain, seal'd in vain. *IV, i, 1*

Music oft hath such a charm
To make bad good, and good provoke to harm. *IV, i, 16*

Every true man's apparel fits your thief. *IV, ii, 46*

The old fantastical duke of dark corners. *IV, iii, 167*

I am a kind of burr; I shall stick. *IV, iii, 193*

We would, and we would not. *IV, iv, 37*

A forted residence 'gainst the tooth of time
And razure of oblivion. *V, i, 12*

Truth is truth
To the end of reckoning. *V, i, 45*

Neither maid, widow, nor wife. *V, i, 173*

Haste still pays haste, and leisure answers leisure,
Like doth quit like, and Measure still for Measure.
V, i, 411

They say best men are molded out of faults,
And, for the most, become much more the better
For being a little bad. *V, i, 440*

What's mine is yours, and what is yours is mine.
V, i, 539

OTHELLO *[1604–1605]*

Horribly stuff'd with epithets of war. *Act I, sc. i, l. 14*

A fellow almost damn'd in a fair wife. *I, i, 21*

The bookish theoric. *I, i, 24*

We cannot all be masters. *I, i, 43*

And when he's old, cashier'd. *I, i, 48*

In following him, I follow but myself. *I, i, 58*

But I will wear my heart upon my sleeve
For daws to peck at. *I, i, 64*

An old black ram
Is tupping your white ewe. *I, i, 88*

You are one of those that will not serve God if the
devil bid you. *I, i, 108*

Your daughter and the Moor are now making the
beast with two backs. *I, i, 117*

Keep up your bright swords, for the dew will rust
them. *I, ii, 59*

The wealthy curled darlings of our nation. *I, ii, 68*

The bloody book of law
You shall yourself read in the bitter letter
After your own sense. *I, iii, 67*

Rude am I in my speech,
And little bless'd with the soft phrase of peace. *I, iii, 81*

Little shall I grace my cause
In speaking for myself. Yet, by your gracious patience,
I will a round unvarnish'd tale deliver
Of my whole course of love. *I, iii,* 88

A maiden never bold;
Of spirit so still and quiet, that her motion
Blush'd at herself. *I, iii,* 94

Still question'd me the story of my life
From year to year, the battles, sieges, fortunes
That I have pass'd. *I, iii,* 129

Wherein I spake of most disastrous chances,
Of moving accidents by flood and field,
Of hair-breadth 'scapes i' the imminent deadly breach.
I, iii, 134

Hills whose heads touch heaven. *I, iii,* 141

And of the Cannibals that each other eat,
The Anthropophagi, and men whose heads
Do grow beneath their shoulders. *I, iii,* 143

My story being done,
She gave me for my pains a world of sighs:
She swore, in faith, 'twas strange, 'twas passing strange;
'Twas pitiful, 'twas wondrous pitiful:
She wish'd she had not heard it, yet she wish'd
That heaven had made her such a man; she thank'd me,
And bade me, if I had a friend that lov'd her,
I should but teach him how to tell my story,
And that would woo her. Upon this hint I spake:
She lov'd me for the dangers I had pass'd,
And I lov'd her that she did pity them.
This only is the witchcraft I have us'd. *I, iii, 158*

I do perceive here a divided duty. *I, iii, 181*

To mourn a mischief that is past and gone
Is the next way to draw new mischief on. *I, iii, 204*

The robb'd that smiles steals something from the
thief. *I, iii, 208*

Our bodies are our gardens, to the which our wills are
gardeners. *I, iii, 324*

Put money in thy purse. *I, iii, 345*

The food that to him now is as luscious as locusts,
shall be to him shortly as bitter as coloquintida.
I, iii, 354

Framed to make women false. *I, iii, 404*

The enchafed flood. *II, i, 17*

One that excels the quirks of blazoning pens. *II, i, 63*

You are pictures out of doors,
Bells in your parlors, wildcats in your kitchens,
Saints in your injuries, devils being offended,
Players in your housewifery, and housewives in
your beds. *II, i, 109*

For I am nothing if not critical. *II, i, 119*

I am not merry, but I do beguile
The thing I am by seeming otherwise. *II, i, 122*

She that was ever fair and never proud,
Had tongue at will and yet was never loud. *II, i, 148*

Iago: To suckle fools and chronicle small beer.
Desdemona: O most lame and impotent conclusion!
II, i, 160

You may relish him more in the soldier than in the
scholar. *II, i, 165*

If it were now to die,
'Twere now to be most happy. *II, i, 192*

Base men being in love have then a nobility in their
natures more than is native to them. *II, i, 218*

Egregiously an ass. *II, i, 321*

I have very poor and unhappy brains for drinking.
II, iii, 34

Potations pottle deep. *II, iii, 57*

Well, God's above all; and there be souls must be
saved, and there be souls must not be saved. *II, iii, 106*

Silence that dreadful bell! it frights the isle
From her propriety. *II, iii, 177*

But men are men; the best sometimes forget. *II, iii, 243*

Thy honesty and love doth mince this matter. *II, iii, 249*

Reputation, reputation, reputation! O! I have lost my reputation. I have lost the immortal part of myself, and what remains is bestial. *II, iii, 264*

Reputation is an idle and most false imposition; oft got without merit, and lost without deserving. *II, iii, 270*

O thou invisible spirit of wine! if thou hast no name to be known by, let us call thee devil! *II, iii, 285*

O God! that men should put an enemy in their mouths to steal away their brains; that we should, with joy, pleasance, revel, and applause, transform ourselves into beasts. *II, iii, 293*

Good wine is a good familiar creature if it be well used. *II, iii, 315*

Play the villain. *II, iii, 345*

How poor are they that have not patience!
What wound did ever heal but by degrees? *II, iii, 379*

Excellent wretch! Perdition catch my soul
But I do love thee! and when I love thee not,
Chaos is come again. *III, iii, 90*

Men should be what they seem. *III, iii, 126*

Speak to me as to thy thinkings,
As thou dost ruminate, and give thy worst of thoughts
The worst of words. *III, iii, 131*

Good name in man and woman, dear my lord,
Is the immediate jewel of their souls:
Who steals my purse steals trash; 'tis
something, nothing;
'Twas mine, 'tis his, and has been slave to thousands;
But he that filches from me my good name
Robs me of that which not enriches him,
And makes me poor indeed. *III, iii, 155*

O! beware, my lord, of jealousy;
It is the green-ey'd monster which doth mock
The meat it feeds on; that cuckold lives in bliss
Who, certain of his fate, loves not his wronger;
But, O! what damned minutes tells he o'er
Who dotes, yet doubts; suspects, yet soundly loves!
III, iii, 165

Poor and content is rich, and rich enough. *III, iii, 172*

Think'st thou I'd make a life of jealousy,
To follow still the changes of the moon
With fresh suspicions? No; to be once in doubt
Is once to be resolved. *III, iii, 177*

I humbly do beseech you of your pardon
For too much loving you. *III, iii, 212*

If I do prove her haggard,
Though that her jesses were my dear heart-strings,
I'd whistle her off and let her down the wind,
To prey at fortune. *III, iii, 260*

I am declin'd
Into the vale of years. *III, iii, 265*

O curse of marriage!
That we can call these delicate creatures ours,
And not their appetites. I had rather be a toad,
And live upon the vapor of a dungeon,
Than keep a corner in the thing I love
For others' uses. *III, iii, 268*

Trifles light as air
Are to the jealous confirmations strong
As proofs of holy writ. *III, iii, 323*

Not poppy, nor mandragora,
Nor all the drowsy syrups of the world,
Shall ever medicine thee to that sweet sleep
Which thou ow'dst yesterday. *III, iii, 331*

He that is robb'd, not wanting what is stol'n,
Let him not know 't and he's not robb'd at all. *III, iii, 343*

O! now, forever
Farewell the tranquil mind; farewell content!
Farewell the plumed troop and the big wars
That make ambition virtue! O, farewell!
Farewell the neighing steed, and the shrill trump,
The spirit-stirring drum, the ear-piercing fife,
The royal banner, and all quality,
Pride, pomp, and circumstance of glorious war!

And, O you mortal engines, whose rude throats
The immortal Jove's dread clamors counterfeit,
Farewell! Othello's occupation's gone! *III, iii,* 348

Be sure of it; give me the ocular proof. *III, iii,* 361

No hinge nor loop
To hang a doubt on. *III, iii,* 366

On horror's head horrors accumulate. *III, iii,* 371

Take note, take note, O world!
To be direct and honest is not safe. *III, iii,* 378

But this denoted a foregone conclusion. *III, iii,* 429

Swell, bosom, with thy fraught,
For 'tis of aspics' tongues! *III, iii,* 450

Like to the Pontick sea,
Whose icy current and compulsive course
Ne'er feels retiring ebb, but keeps due on
To the Propontic and the Hellespont,
Even so my bloody thoughts, with violent pace,
Shall ne'er look back, ne'er ebb to humble love,
Till that a capable and wide revenge
Swallow them up. *III, iii,* 454

Our new heraldry is hands not hearts. *III, iv, 48*

But jealous souls will not be answer'd so;
They are not ever jealous for the cause,
But jealous for they are jealous; 'tis a monster
Begot upon itself, born on itself. *III, iv, 158*

'Tis the strumpet's plague
To beguile many and be beguil'd by one. *IV, i, 97*

They laugh that win. *IV, i, 123*

My heart is turned to stone; I strike it, and it hurts
my hand. O! the world hath not a sweeter creature;
she might lie by an emperor's side and command
him tasks. *IV, i, 190*

O, she will sing the savageness out of a bear. *IV, i, 198*

But yet the pity of it, Iago! O! Iago, the pity of it,
Iago! *IV, i, 205*

Is this the noble nature
Whom passion could not shake? whose solid virtue
The shot of accident nor dart of chance
Could neither graze nor pierce? *IV, i, 276*

I understand a fury in your words,
But not the words. *IV, ii, 31*

Steep'd me in poverty to the very lips. *IV, ii, 49*

But, alas! to make me
A fixed figure for the time of scorn
To point his slow and moving finger at. *IV, ii, 52*

Patience, thou young and rose-lipp'd cherubin. *IV, ii, 62*

O thou weed!
Who art so lovely fair and smell'st so sweet
That the sense aches at thee, would thou hadst ne'er
been born. *IV, ii, 66*

O heaven! that such companions thou'dst unfold,
And put in every honest hand a whip
To lash the rascals naked through the world. *IV, ii, 141*

Unkindness may do much;
And his unkindness may defeat my life,
But never taint my love. *IV, ii, 159*

The poor soul sat sighing by a sycamore tree,
Sing all a green willow;
Her hand on her bosom, her head on her knee,
Sing willow, willow, willow. *IV, iii, 41*

It makes us, or it mars us. *V, i, 4*

Every way makes my gain. *V, i, 14*

He hath a daily beauty in his life. *V, i, 19*

This is the night
That either makes me or fordoes me quite. *V, i, 128*

And smooth as monumental alabaster. *V, ii, 5*

Put out the light, and then put out the light:
If I quench thee, thou flaming minister,
I can again thy former light restore,
Should I repent me; but once put out thy light,
Thou cunning'st pattern of excelling nature,
I know not where is that Promethean heat
That can thy light relume. *V, ii, 7*

It is the very error of the moon;
She comes more near the earth than she was wont,
And makes men mad. *V, ii, 107*

She was as false as water. *V, ii, 132*

Curse his better angel from his side,
And fall to reprobation. *V, ii, 206*

Here is my journey's end, here is my butt,
And very sea-mark of my utmost sail. *V, ii, 266*

An honorable murderer, if you will;
For nought I did in hate, but all in honor.
V, ii, 293

I have done the state some service, and they know 't;
No more of that. I pray you, in your letters,
When you shall these unlucky deeds relate,
Speak of me as I am; nothing extenuate,
Nor set down aught in malice: then, must you speak
Of one that lov'd not wisely but too well;
Of one not easily jealous, but, being wrought,
Perplex'd in the extreme; of one whose hand,
Like the base Indian, threw a pearl away
Richer than all his tribe; of one whose subdu'd eyes

Albeit unused to the melting mood,
Drop tears as fast as the Arabian trees
Their med'cinable gum. *V, ii, 338*

In Aleppo once,
Where a malignant and a turban'd Turk
Beat a Venetian and traduc'd the state,
I took by the throat the circumcised dog,
And smote him thus. *V, ii, 354*

KING LEAR [1605]

My love's
More richer than my tongue. *Act I, sc. i, l. 79*

Now, our joy,
Although our last, not least. *I, i, 84*

Nothing will come of nothing. *I, i, 92*

Mend your speech a little,
Lest you may mar your fortunes. *I, i, 96*

Lear: So young, and so untender?
Cordelia: So young, my lord, and true. *I, i, 108*

Come not between the dragon and his wrath. *I, i,* 124

Kill thy physician, and the fee bestow
Upon the foul disease. *I, i,* 166

I want that glib and oily art
To speak and purpose not. *I, i,* 227

A still-soliciting eye. *I, i,* 234

Time shall unfold what plighted cunning hides;
Who covers faults, at last shame them derides.
I, i, 282

The infirmity of his age. *I, i,* 296

Who in the lusty stealth of nature take
More composition and fierce quality
Than doth, within a dull, stale, tired bed,
Go to the creating a whole tribe of fops. *I, ii,* 11

Now, gods, stand up for bastards! *I, ii,* 22

We have seen the best of our time: machinations,
hollowness, treachery, and all ruinous disorders,
follow us disquietly to our graves. *I, ii,* 125

This is the excellent foppery of the world, that, when
we are sick in fortune, — often the surfeit of our own
behavior, — we make guilty of our disasters the sun,
the moon, and the stars; as if we were villains by
necessity, fools by heavenly compulsion, knaves,
thieves, and treachers by spherical predominance,
drunkards, liars, and adulterers by an enforced
obedience of planetary influence. *I, ii,* 129

Edgar —
[*Enter Edgar*]
and pat he comes, like the catastrophe of the old
comedy: my cue is villainous melancholy, with a sigh
like Tom o' Bedlam. *I, ii,* 149

Lear: Dost thou know me, fellow?
Kent: No, sir, but you have that in your countenance
which I would fain call master.
Lear: What's that?
Kent: Authority. *I, iv,* 28

That which ordinary men are fit for, I am qualified in,
and the best of me is diligence. *I, iv,* 36

Truth's a dog must to kennel; he must be whipped out
when Lady the brach may stand by the fire and stink.

I, iv, 125

> Have more than thou showest,
> Speak less than thou knowest,
> Lend less than thou owest. I, iv, 132

Can you make no use of nothing, nuncle? I, iv, 144

> Ingratitude, thou marble-hearted fiend,
> More hideous, when thou show'st thee in a child,
> Than the sea-monster. I, iv, 283

> How sharper than a serpent's tooth it is
> To have a thankless child! I, iv, 312

Striving to better, oft we mar what's well. I, iv, 371

The son and heir of a mongrel bitch. II, ii, 23

> I have seen better faces in my time
> Than stands on any shoulder that I see
> Before me at this instant. II, ii, 99

A good man's fortune may grow out at heels. *II, ii, 164*

Fortune, good night, smile once more; turn thy wheel!
II, ii, 180

Hysterica passio! down, thou climbing sorrow!
Thy element's below. *II, iv, 57*

That sir which serves and seeks for gain,
And follows but for form,
Will pack when it begins to rain,
And leave thee in the storm. *II, iv, 79*

Nature in you stands on the very verge
Of her confine. *II, iv, 149*

Necessity's sharp pinch! *II, iv, 214*

Our basest beggars
Are in the poorest thing superfluous:
Allow not nature more than nature needs,
Man's life is cheap as beast's. *II, iv, 267*

Let not women's weapons, waterdrops,
Stain my man's cheeks! *II, iv, 280*

I have full cause of weeping, but this heart
Shall break into a hundred thousand flaws
Or ere I'll weep. O fool! I shall go mad. *II, iv,* 287

Blow, winds, and crack your cheeks! rage! blow!
You cataracts and hurricanoes, spout
Till you have drench'd our steeples, drown'd the cocks!
You sulphurous and thought-executing fires,
Vaunt-couriers to oak-cleaving thunderbolts,
Singe my white head! And thou, all-shaking thunder,
Strike flat the thick rotundity o' the world!
Crack nature's molds, all germens spill at once
That make ingrateful man! *III, ii,* 1

I tax not you, you elements, with unkindness. *III, ii,* 16

A poor, infirm, weak, and despis'd old man. *III, ii,* 20

There was never yet fair woman but she made mouths
in a glass. *III, ii,* 35

I will be the pattern of all patience. *III, ii,* 37

I am a man
More sinn'd against than sinning. *III, ii,* 59

The art of our necessities is strange,
That can make vile things precious. *III, ii, 70*

He that has and a little tiny wit,
With hey, ho, the wind and the rain,
Must make content with his fortunes fit,
Though the rain it raineth every day. *III, ii, 76*

O! that way madness lies; let me shun that. *III, iv, 21*

Poor naked wretches, wheresoe'er you are,
That bide the pelting of this pitiless storm,
How shall your houseless heads and unfed sides,
Your loop'd and window'd raggedness, defend you
From seasons such as these? O! I have ta'en
Too little care of this. Take physic, pomp;
Expose thyself to feel what wretches feel,
That thou mayst shake the superflux to them,
And show the heavens more just. *III, iv, 28*

Pillicock sat on Pillicock-hill:
Halloo, halloo, loo, loo! *III, iv, 75*

Out-paramoured the Turk. *III, iv, 91*

Is man no more than this? Consider him well. Thou
owest the worm no silk, the beast no hide, the sheep
no wool, the cat no perfume. Ha! here's three on 's are
sophisticated; thou art the thing itself;
unaccommodated man is no more but such a poor,
bare, forked animal as thou art. Off, off, you lendings!
Come; unbutton here.   *III, iv, 105*

'Tis a naughty night to swim in.   *III, iv, 113*

The green mantle of the standing pool.   *III, iv, 137*

But mice and rats and such small deer
Have been Tom's food for seven long year.   *III, iv, 142*

The prince of darkness is a gentleman.   *III, iv, 147*

Poor Tom's a-cold.   *III, iv, 151*

Child Rowland to the dark tower came,
His word was still, Fie, foh, and fum,
I smell the blood of a British man.   *III, iv, 185*

He's mad that trusts in the tameness of a wolf, a
horse's health, a boy's love, or a whore's oath. *III, vi,* 20

The little dogs and all,
Tray, Blanch, and Sweetheart, see, they bark at me.
III, vi, 65

Is there any cause in nature that makes these hard
hearts? *III, vi,* 81

I am tied to the stake, and I must stand the course.
III, vii, 54

Out, vile jelly! *III, vii,* 83

The lowest and most dejected thing of fortune. *IV, i,* 3

The worst is not,
So long as we can say, "This is the worst." *IV, i,* 27

As flies to wanton boys, are we to the gods;
They kill us for their sport. *IV, i,* 36

You are not worth the dust which the rude wind
Blows in your face. *IV, ii,* 30

She that herself will sliver and disbranch
From her material sap, perforce must wither
And come to deadly use. *IV, ii,* 34

Wisdom and goodness to the vile seem vile;
Filths savor but themselves. *IV, ii,* 38

Tigers, not daughters. *IV, ii,* 39

It is the stars,
The stars above us, govern our conditions.
IV, iii, 34

Our foster-nurse of nature is repose. *IV, iv,* 12

How fearful
And dizzy 'tis to cast one's eyes so low!
The crows and choughs that wing the midway air
Show scarce so gross as beetles; halfway down
Hangs one that gathers samphire, dreadful trade!
Methinks he seems no bigger than his head.
The fishermen that walk upon the beach
Appear like mice, and yond tall anchoring bark
Diminish'd to her cock, her cock a buoy
Almost too small for sight. The murmuring surge,

That on the unnumber'd idle pebbles chafes,
Cannot be heard so high. *IV, vi,* 12

Nature's above art in that respect. *IV, vi,* 87

Ay, every inch a king. *IV, vi,* 110

The wren goes to 't, and the small gilded fly
Does lecher in my sight.
Let copulation thrive. *IV, vi,* 115

Give me an ounce of civet, good apothecary, to
sweeten my imagination. *IV, vi,* 133

A man may see how this world goes with no eyes.
Look with thine ears: see how yond justice rails upon
yon simple thief. Hark, in thine ear: change places;
and, handy-dandy, which is the justice,
which is the thief? *IV, vi,* 154

Through tatter'd clothes small vices do appear;
Robes and furr'd gowns hide all. Plate sin with gold,
And the strong lance of justice hurtless breaks;
Arm it in rags, a pigmy's straw does pierce it. *IV, vi,* 169

Get thee glass eyes;
And, like a scurvy politician, seem
To see the things thou dost not. *IV, vi,* 175

When we are born, we cry that we are come
To this great stage of fools. *IV, vi,* 187

Then, kill, kill, kill, kill, kill, kill! *IV, vi,* 192

Mine enemy's dog,
Though he had bit me, should have stood that night
Against my fire. *IV, vii,* 36

Thou art a soul in bliss; but I am bound
Upon a wheel of fire, that mine own tears
Do scald like molten lead. *IV, vii,* 46

I am a very foolish fond old man,
Fourscore and upward, not an hour more or less;
And, to deal plainly,
I fear I am not in my perfect mind. *IV, vii,* 60

Pray you now, forget and forgive. *IV, vii,* 84

Men must endure
Their going hence, even as their coming hither:
Ripeness is all. *V, ii, 9*

Come, let's away to prison;
We two alone will sing like birds i' the cage:
When thou dost ask me blessing, I'll kneel down,
And ask of thee forgiveness: so we'll live,
And pray, and sing, and tell old tales, and laugh
At gilded butterflies, and hear poor rogues
Talk of court news; and we'll talk with them too,
Who loses and who wins; who's in, who's out;
And take upon's the mystery of things,
As if we were God's spies: and we'll wear out,
In a wall'd prison, packs and sets of great ones
That ebb and flow by the moon. *V, iii, 8*

Upon such sacrifices, my Cordelia,
The gods themselves throw incense. *V, iii, 20*

The gods are just, and of our pleasant vices
Make instruments to plague us. *V, iii, 172*

The wheel is come full circle. *V, iii, 176*

Howl, howl, howl, howl! O! you are men of stones:
Had I your tongues and eyes, I'd use them so
That heaven's vaults should crack. She's gone forever.
V, iii, 259

Her voice was ever soft,
Gentle and low, an excellent thing in woman. *V, iii, 274*

And my poor fool is hang'd! No, no, no life!
Why should a dog, a horse, a rat, have life,
And thou no breath at all? Thou'lt come no more,
Never, never, never, never, never!
Pray you, undo this button. *V, iii, 307*

Vex not his ghost: O! let him pass; he hates him
That would upon the rack of this tough world
Stretch him out longer. *V, iii, 315*

The weight of this sad time we must obey;
Speak what we feel, not what we ought to say.
The oldest hath borne most: we that are young,
Shall never see so much, nor live so long. *V, iii, 325*

TIMON OF ATHENS [1605–1608]

'Tis not enough to help the feeble up,
But to support him after.   *Act I, sc. i, l.* 108

I call the gods to witness.   *I, i,* 138

I wonder men dare trust themselves with men.   *I, ii,* 45

Here's that which is too weak to be a sinner,
Honest water, which ne'er left man i' the mire.   *I, ii,* 60

Immortal gods, I crave no pelf;
I pray for no man but myself:
Grant I may never prove so fond,
To trust man on his oath or bond.   *I, ii,* 64

Men shut their doors against a setting sun.   *I, ii,* 152

Every man has his fault, and honesty is his.   *III, i,* 30

Nothing emboldens sin so much as mercy.   *III, v,* 3

You fools of fortune, trencher-friends, time's flies.
III, vi, 107

We have seen better days. *IV, ii, 27*

O! the fierce wretchedness that glory brings us.
IV, ii, 30

I am Misanthropos, and hate mankind. *IV, iii, 53*

Life's uncertain voyage. *V, i, 207*

MACBETH [1606]

First Witch: When shall we three meet again
In thunder, lightning, or in rain?
Second Witch: When the hurlyburly's done,
When the battle's lost and won. *Act 1, sc. i, l. 1*

Fair is foul, and foul is fair:
Hover through the fog and filthy air. *I, i, 12*

Banners flout the sky. *I, ii, 50*

A sailor's wife had chestnuts in her lap,
And munch'd, and munch'd, and munch'd:
"Give me," quoth I:
"Aroint thee, witch!" the rump-fed ronyon cries. *I, iii, 4*

Sleep shall neither night nor day
Hang upon his pent-house lid. *I, iii, 19*

Dwindle, peak, and pine. *I, iii, 23*

The weird sisters, hand in hand,
Posters of the sea and land,
Thus do go about, about:
Thrice to thine, and thrice to mine,
And thrice again, to make up nine.
Peace! The charm's wound up. *I, iii, 32*

So foul and fair a day I have not seen. *I, iii, 38*

If you can look into the seeds of time,
And say which grain will grow and which will not,
Speak. *I, iii, 58*

And to be king
Stands not within the prospect of belief. *I, iii, 73*

The earth hath bubbles, as the water has,
And these are of them. *I, iii,* 79

Or have we eaten on the insane root
That takes the reason prisoner? *I, iii,* 84

And oftentimes, to win us to our harm,
The instruments of darkness tell us truths,
Win us with honest trifles, to betray 's
In deepest consequence. *I, iii,* 123

As happy prologues to the swelling act
Of the imperial theme. *I, iii,* 128

I am Thane of Cawdor:
If good, why do I yield to that suggestion
Whose horrid image doth unfix my hair
And make my seated heart knock at my ribs,
Against the use of nature? Present fears
Are less than horrible imaginings. *I, iii,* 134

If chance will have me king,
why, chance may crown me,
Without my stir. *I, iii,* 143

Come what come may,
Time and the hour runs through the roughest day.
I, iii, 146

Nothing in his life
Became him like the leaving it; he died
As one that had been studied in his death
To throw away the dearest thing he ow'd,
As 'twere a careless trifle. *I, iv, 7*

There's no art
To find the mind's construction in the face:
He was a gentleman on whom I built
An absolute trust. *I, iv, 11*

Glamis thou art, and Cawdor; and shalt be
What thou art promis'd. Yet do I fear thy nature;
It is too full o' the milk of human kindness
To catch the nearest way. *I, v, 16*

The raven himself is hoarse
That croaks the fatal entrance of Duncan
Under my battlements. Come, you spirits
That tend on mortal thoughts! unsex me here,
And fill me from the crown to the toe top full
Of direst cruelty; make thick my blood,
Stop up the access and passage to remorse,

That no compunctious visitings of nature
Shake my fell purpose, nor keep peace between
The effect and it! Come to my woman's breasts,
And take my milk for gall, you murdering ministers.
I, v, 38

Nor heaven peep through the blanket of the dark,
To cry, "Hold, hold!" I, v, 54

Your face, my thane, is as a book where men
May read strange matters. I, v, 63

Look like the innocent flower,
But be the serpent under 't. I, v, 66

Duncan: This castle hath a pleasant seat; the air
Nimbly and sweetly recommends itself
Unto our gentle senses.
Banquo: This guest of summer,
The temple-haunting martlet, does approve
By his lov'd mansionry that the heaven's breath
Smells wooingly here: no jutty, frieze,
Buttress, nor coign of vantage, but this bird
Hath made his pendent bed and procreant cradle:
Where they most breed and haunt, I have observ'd
The air is delicate. I, vi, 1

If it were done when 'tis done, then 'twere well
It were done quickly; if the assassination
Could trammel up the consequence, and catch
With his surcease success; that but this blow
Might be the be-all and the end-all here,
But here, upon this bank and shoal of time,
We'd jump the life to come. *I, vii, 1*

This even-handed justice. *I, vii, 10*

Besides, this Duncan
Hath borne his faculties so meek, hath been
So clear in his great office, that his virtues
Will plead like angels trumpet-tongu'd against
The deep damnation of his taking-off;
And pity, like a naked new-born babe,
Striding the blast, or heaven's cherubin, hors'd
Upon the sightless couriers of the air,
Shall blow the horrid deed in every eye,
That tears shall drown the wind. I have no spur
To prick the sides of my intent, but only
Vaulting ambition, which o'erleaps itself
And falls on the other. *I, vii, 16*

I have bought
Golden opinions from all sorts of people. *I, vii, 32*

Letting "I dare not" wait upon "I would,"
Like the poor cat i' the adage. *I, vii,* 44

I dare do all that may become a man;
Who dares do more is none. *I, vii,* 46

Nor time nor place
Did then adhere. *I, vii,* 51

I have given suck, and know
How tender 'tis to love the babe that milks me:
I would, while it was smiling in my face,
Have pluck'd my nipple from his boneless gums,
And dash'd the brains out, had I so sworn as you
Have done to this. *I, vii,* 54

Macbeth: If we should fail —
Lady Macbeth: We fail!
But screw your courage to the sticking-place,
And we'll not fail. *I, vii,* 59

Memory, the warder of the brain. *I, vii,* 65

Away, and mock the time with fairest show:
False face must hide what the false heart doth know.

I, vii, 81

The moon is down. *II, i, 2*

There's husbandry in heaven;
Their candles are all out. *II, i, 4*

Merciful powers!
Restrain in me the cursed thoughts that nature
Gives way to in repose. *II, i, 7*

Shut up
In measureless content. *II, i, 16*

Is this a dagger which I see before me,
The handle toward my hand? Come, let me clutch thee:
I have thee not, and yet I see thee still.
Art thou not, fatal vision, sensible
To feeling as to sight? or art thou but
A dagger of the mind, a false creation,
Proceeding from the heat-oppressed brain? *II, i, 33*

Now o'er the one half-world
Nature seems dead, and wicked dreams abuse
The curtain'd sleep; witchcraft celebrates
Pale Hecate's offerings. *II, i, 49*

Thou sure and firm-set earth,
Hear not my steps, which way they walk, for fear
The very stones prate of my whereabout. *II, i, 56*

The bell invites me.
Hear it not, Duncan; for it is a knell
That summons thee to heaven or to hell. *II, i, 62*

It was the owl that shriek'd, the fatal bellman,
Which gives the stern'st good-night. *II, ii, 4*

The attempt and not the deed
Confounds us. *II, ii, 12*

Had he not resembled
My father as he slept I had done 't. *II, ii, 14*

I had most need of blessing, and "Amen"
Stuck in my throat. *II, ii, 33*

Methought I heard a voice cry "Sleep no more!
Macbeth does murder sleep," the innocent sleep,
Sleep that knits up the ravell'd sleave of care,
The death of each day's life, sore labor's bath,
Balm of hurt minds, great nature's second course,
Chief nourisher in life's feast. *II, ii, 36*

Glamis hath murder'd sleep, and therefore Cawdor
Shall sleep no more, Macbeth shall sleep no more!
II, ii, 43

Infirm of purpose!
Give me the daggers. The sleeping and the dead
Are but as pictures; 'tis the eye of childhood
That fears a painted devil. *II, ii, 53*

Will all great Neptune's ocean wash this blood
Clean from my hand? No, this my hand will rather
The multitudinous seas incarnadine,
Making the green one red. *II, ii, 61*

The primrose way to the everlasting bonfire. *II, iii, 22*

It [drink] provokes the desire, but it takes away the
performance. *II, iii, 34*

The labor we delight in physics pain. *II, iii, 56*

Confusion now hath made his masterpiece!
Most sacrilegious murder hath broke ope
The Lord's anointed temple, and stole thence
The life o' the building! *II, iii, 72*

Shake off this downy sleep, death's counterfeit. *II, iii,* 83

Had I but died an hour before this chance
I had liv'd a blessed time; for, from this instant,
There's nothing serious in mortality,
All is but toys; renown and grace is dead,
The wine of life is drawn, and the mere lees
Is left this vault to brag of. *II, iii,* 98

Who can be wise, amaz'd, temperate and furious,
Loyal and neutral, in a moment? No man. *II, iii,* 115

To show an unfelt sorrow is an office
Which the false man does easy. *II, iii,* 143

A falcon, towering in her pride of place,
Was by a mousing owl hawk'd at and kill'd. *II, iv,* 12

I must become a borrower of the night
For a dark hour or twain. *III, i,* 27

To be thus is nothing;
But to be safely thus. *III, i,* 48

Murderer: We are men, my liege.
Macbeth: Ay, in the catalogue ye go for men. *III, i, 91*

I am one, my liege,
Whom the vile blows and buffets of the world
Have so incens'd that I am reckless what
I do to spite the world. *III, i, 108*

So weary with disasters, tugg'd with fortune,
That I would set my life on any chance,
To mend it or be rid on 't. *III, i, 112*

Things without all remedy
Should be without regard: what's done is done. *III, ii, 11*

We have scotch'd the snake, not kill'd it. *III, ii, 13*

Duncan is in his grave;
After life's fitful fever he sleeps well;
Treason has done his worst: nor steel, nor poison,
Malice domestic, foreign levy, nothing
Can touch him further. *III, ii, 22*

Then be thou jocund. Ere the bat hath flown
His cloister'd flight, ere, to black Hecate's summons
The shard-borne beetle with his drowsy hums
Hath rung night's yawning peal, there shall be done
A deed of dreadful note. *III, ii,* 40

Come, seeling night,
Scarf up the tender eye of pitiful day,
And with thy bloody and invisible hand
Cancel and tear to pieces that great bond
Which keeps me pale! Light thickens, and the crow
Makes wing to the rooky wood. *III, ii,* 46

Now spurs the lated traveler apace
To gain the timely inn. *III, iii,* 6

But now I am cabin'd, cribb'd, confin'd, bound in
To saucy doubts and fears. *III, iv,* 24

Now good digestion wait on appetite,
And health on both! *III, iv,* 38

Thou canst not say I did it: never shake
Thy gory locks at me. *III, iv,* 50

The air-drawn dagger. *III, iv, 62*

I drink to the general joy of the whole table. *III, iv, 89*

What man dare, I dare:
Approach thou like the rugged Russian bear,
The arm'd rhinoceros, or the Hyrcan tiger;
Take any shape but that, and my firm nerves
Shall never tremble. *III, iv, 99*

Hence, horrible shadow!
Unreal mockery, hence! *III, iv, 106*

Stand not upon the order of your going,
But go at once. *III, iv, 119*

It will have blood, they say; blood will have blood:
Stones have been known to move and trees to speak.
III, iv, 122

Macbeth: What is the night?
Lady Macbeth: Almost at odds with morning, which is
which. *III, iv, 126*

I am in blood
Stepp'd in so far, that, should I wade no more,
Returning were as tedious as go o'er. *III, iv,* 136

Double, double toil and trouble;
Fire burn and cauldron bubble. *IV, i,* 10

Eye of newt, and toe of frog,
Wool of bat, and tongue of dog. *IV, i,* 14

Finger of birth-strangled babe,
Ditch-deliver'd by a drab. *IV, i,* 30

By the pricking of my thumbs,
Something wicked this way comes.
Open, locks,
Whoever knocks! *IV, i,* 44

How now, you secret, black, and midnight hags!
IV, i, 48

A deed without a name. *IV, i,* 49

Be bloody, bold, and resolute; laugh to scorn
The power of man, for none of woman born
Shall harm Macbeth. *IV, i, 79*

But yet I'll make assurance double sure,
And take a bond of fate. *IV, i, 83*

Macbeth shall never vanquish'd be until
Great Birnam wood to high Dunsinane hill
Shall come against him. *IV, i, 92*

Show his eyes, and grieve his heart;
Come like shadows, so depart. *IV, i, 110*

What! will the line stretch out to the crack of doom?
IV, i, 117

When our actions do not,
Our fears do make us traitors. *IV, ii, 3*

He wants the natural touch. *IV, ii, 9*

Angels are bright still, though the brightest fell.
IV, iii, 22

Pour the sweet milk of concord into hell,
Uproar the universal peace, confound
All unity on earth. *IV, iii, 98*

Give sorrow words; the grief that does not speak
Whispers the o'er-fraught heart and bids it break.
IV, iii, 209

All my pretty ones?
Did you say all? O hell-kite! All?
What! all my pretty chickens and their dam
At one fell swoop? *IV, iii, 216*

Malcolm: Dispute it like a man.
Macduff: I shall do so;
But I must also feel it as a man:
I cannot but remember such things were,
That were most precious to me. *IV, iii, 219*

Out, damned spot! out, I say! *V, i, 38*

Fie, my lord, fie! a soldier, and afeard? *V, i, 40*

Who would have thought the old man to have had so
much blood in him? *V, i, 42*

The Thane of Fife had a wife: where is she now?
V, i, 46

All the perfumes of Arabia will not sweeten this little
hand. *V, i, 56*

Those he commands move only in command,
Nothing in love; now does he feel his title
Hang loose about him, like a giant's robe
Upon a dwarfish thief. *V, ii, 19*

The devil damn thee black, thou cream-fac'd loon!
Where gott'st thou that goose look? *V, iii, 11*

Thou lily-liver'd boy. *V, iii, 15*

I have liv'd long enough: my way of life
Is fall'n into the sere, the yellow leaf;
And that which should accompany old age,
As honor, love, obedience, troops of friends,
I must not look to have; but, in their stead,
Curses, not loud but deep, mouth-honor, breath,
Which the poor heart would fain deny, and dare not.
V, iii, 22

Macbeth: Canst thou not minister to a mind diseas'd,
Pluck from the memory a rooted sorrow,
Raze out the written troubles of the brain,
And with some sweet oblivious antidote
Cleanse the stuff'd bosom of that perilous stuff
Which weighs upon the heart?
Doctor: Therein the patient
Must minister to himself.
Macbeth: Throw physic to the dogs; I'll none of it.
V, iii, 40

I would applaud thee to the very echo,
That should applaud again. *V, iii, 53*

Hang out our banners on the outward walls;
The cry is still, "They come"; our castle's strength
Will laugh a siege to scorn. *V, v, 1*

My fell of hair
Would at a dismal treatise rouse and stir
As life were in 't. I have supp'd full with horrors. *V, v, 11*

She should have died hereafter;
There would have been a time for such a word.
Tomorrow, and tomorrow, and tomorrow,
Creeps in this petty pace from day to day,
To the last syllable of recorded time;

And all our yesterdays have lighted fools
The way to dusty death. Out, out, brief candle!
Life's but a walking shadow, a poor player
That struts and frets his hour upon the stage,
And then is heard no more; it is a tale
Told by an idiot, full of sound and fury,
Signifying nothing. *V, v, 17*

I 'gin to be aweary of the sun,
And wish the estate o' the world were now undone.
V, v, 49

Blow, wind! come, wrack!
At least we'll die with harness on our back. *V, v, 51*

Why should I play the Roman fool; and die
On mine own sword? *V, vii, 30*

I bear a charmed life. *V, vii, 41*

Macduff was from his mother's womb
Untimely ripp'd. *V, vii, 44*

And be these juggling fiends no more believ'd,
That palter with us in a double sense;
That keep the word of promise to our ear
And break it to our hope. *V, vii,* 48

Live to be the show and gaze o' the time. *V, vii,* 53

Lay on, Macduff,
And damn'd be him that first cries, "Hold, enough!"
V, vii, 62

ANTONY AND CLEOPATRA [1606–1607]

You shall see in him
The triple pillar of the world transform'd
Into a strumpet's fool. *Act 1, sc. i, l.* 12

There's beggary in the love that can be reckon'd. *I, i,* 15

Let Rome in Tiber melt, and the wide arch
Of the rang'd empire fall! Here is my space.
Kingdoms are clay. *I, i,* 33

In nature's infinite book of secrecy
A little I can read. *I, ii, 11*

I love long life better than figs. *I, ii, 34*

On the sudden
A Roman thought hath struck him. *I, ii, 90*

Eternity was in our lips and eyes,
Bliss in our brows bent. *I, iii, 35*

Good now, play one scene
Of excellent dissembling, and let it look
Like perfect honor. *I, iii, 78*

O! my oblivion is a very Antony,
And I am all forgotten. *I, iii, 90*

Give me to drink mandragora. . . .
That I might sleep out this great gap of time
My Antony is away. *I, v, 4*

O happy horse, to bear the weight of Antony! *I, v, 21*

The demi-Atlas of this earth, the arm
And burgonet of men. *I, v,* 23

Where's my serpent of old Nile? *I, v,* 25

A morsel for a monarch. *I, v,* 31

My man of men. *I, v,* 71

My salad days,
When I was green in judgment. *I, v,* 73

We, ignorant of ourselves,
Beg often our own harms, which the wise powers
Deny us for our good; so find we profit
By losing of our prayers. *II, i,* 5

Epicurean cooks
Sharpen with cloyless sauce his appetite. *II, i,* 24

No worse a husband than the best of men. *II, ii,* 135

The barge she sat in, like a burnish'd throne,
Burn'd on the water; the poop was beaten gold,
Purple the sails, and so perfumed, that
The winds were love-sick with them;
the oars were silver,
Which to the tune of flutes kept stroke, and made
The water which they beat to follow faster,
As amorous of their strokes. For her own person,
It beggar'd all description. *II, ii, 199*

Age cannot wither her, nor custom stale
Her infinite variety; other women cloy
The appetites they feed, but she makes hungry
Where most she satisfies; for vilest things
Become themselves in her, that the holy priests
Bless her when she is riggish. *II, ii, 243*

I have not kept my square, but that to come
Shall all be done by the rule. *II, iii, 6*

I will to Egypt
And though I make this marriage for my peace,
I' the East my pleasure lies. *II, iii, 38*

Music, moody food
Of us that trade in love. *II, v, 1*

Though it be honest, it is never good
To bring bad news. *II, v,* 85

He will to his Egyptian dish again. *II, vi,* 133

Come, thou monarch of the vine,
Plumpy Bacchus, with pink eyne! *II, vii,* 120

Ambition,
The soldier's virtue. *III, i,* 22

Celerity is never more admir'd
Than by the negligent. *III, vii,* 24

We have kiss'd away
Kingdoms and provinces. *III, viii,* 17

He wears the rose
Of youth upon him. *III, xi,* 20

Men's judgments are
A parcel of their fortunes, and things outward
Do draw the inward quality after them,
To suffer all alike. *III, xi,* 31

I found you as a morsel, cold upon
Dead Caesar's trencher. *III, xi, 116*

Let's have one other gaudy night. *III, xi, 182*

Now he'll outstare the lightning. To be furious
Is to be frighted out of fear. *III, xi, 194*

To business that we love we rise betime,
And go to 't with delight. *IV, iv, 20*

O infinite virtue! com'st thou smiling from
The world's great snare uncaught? *IV, viii, 17*

The shirt of Nessus is upon me. *IV, x, 56*

Sometimes we see a cloud that's dragonish;
A vapor sometime like a bear or lion,
A tower'd citadel, a pendant rock,
A forked mountain, or blue promontory
With trees upon 't. *IV, xii, 2*

Unarm, Eros; the long day's task is done,
And we must sleep. *IV, xii, 35*

But I will be
A bridegroom in my death, and run into 't
As to a lover's bed. *IV, xii,* 99

O sun!
Burn the great sphere thou mov'st in; darkling stand
The varying shore o' the world. *IV, xiii,* 10

I am dying, Egypt, dying; only
I here importune death awhile, until
Of many thousand kisses the poor last
I lay upon thy lips. *IV, xiii,* 18

O! wither'd is the garland of the war,
The soldier's pole is fall'n; young boys and girls
Are level now with men; the odds is gone,
And there is nothing left remarkable
Beneath the visiting moon. *IV, xiii,* 64

Let's do it after the high Roman fashion,
And make death proud to take us. *IV, xiii,* 87

And it is great
To do that thing that ends all other deeds,
Which shackles accidents, and bolts up change. *V, ii,* 4

His legs bestrid the ocean; his rear'd arm
Crested the world; his voice was propertied
As all the tuned spheres, and that to friends;
But when he meant to quail and shake the orb,
He was as rattling thunder. For his bounty,
There was no winter in 't, an autumn 'twas
That grew the more by reaping; his delights
Were dolphin-like, they show'd his back above
The element they liv'd in; in his livery
Walk'd crowns and crownets, realms and islands were
As plates dropp'd from his pocket. *V, ii,* 82

The bright day is done,
And we are for the dark. *V, ii,* 192

The quick comedians
Extemporally will stage us, and present
Our Alexandrian revels. Antony
Shall be brought drunken forth, and I shall see
Some squeaking Cleopatra boy my greatness
I' the posture of a whore. *V, ii,* 215

A woman is a dish for the gods, if the devil dress
her not. *V, ii,* 274

I wish you joy of the worm. *V, ii,* 280

I have
Immortal longings in me. *V, ii,* 282

Husband, I come. *V, ii,* 289

If thou and nature can so gently part,
The stroke of death is as a lover's pinch,
Which hurts, and is desir'd. *V, ii,* 296

Dost thou not see my baby at my breast,
That sucks the nurse asleep? *V, ii,* 311

Now boast thee, death, in thy possession lies
A lass unparallel'd. *V, ii,* 317

First Guard: . . . Charmian, is this well done?
Charmian: It is well done, and fitting for a princess
Descended of so many royal kings. *V, ii,* 327

As she would catch another Antony
In her strong toil of grace. *V, ii,* 348

CORIOLANUS [1607–1608]

The gods sent not
Corn for the rich men only.   *Act 1, sc. i, l. 213*

They threw their caps
As they would hang them on the horns o' the moon,
Shouting their emulation.   *I, i, 218*

All the yarn she spun in Ulysses' absence did but fill
Ithaca full of moths.   *I, iii, 93*

Nature teaches beasts to know their friends.   *II, i, 6*

A cup of hot wine with not a drop of allaying Tiber in 't.
II, i, 52

My gracious silence, hail!   *II, i, 194*

He himself stuck not to call us the many-headed
multitude.   *II, iii, 18*

Bid them wash their faces,
And keep their teeth clean.   *II, iii, 65*

I thank you for your voices, thank you,
    Your most sweet voices. *II, iii, 179*

The mutable, rank-scented many. *III, i, 65*

Hear you this Triton of the minnows? mark you
    His absolute "shall"? *III, i, 88*

What is the city but the people? *III, i, 198*

His nature is too noble for the world:
He would not flatter Neptune for his trident,
Or Jove for 's power to thunder. His heart's his mouth:
What his breast forges, that his tongue must vent.
                    III, i, 254

The beast
With many heads butts me away. *IV, i, 1*

O! a kiss
Long as my exile, sweet as my revenge! *V, iii, 44*

Chaste as the icicle
That's curdied by the frost from purest snow,
    And hangs on Dian's temple. *V, iii, 65*

He wants nothing of a god but eternity and a heaven
to throne in. *V, iv, 25*

They'll give him death by inches. *V, iv, 43*

If you have writ your annals true, 'tis there,
That, like an eagle in a dovecote, I
Flutter'd your Volscians in Corioli:
Alone I did it. *V, v, 114*

Thou hast done a deed whereat valor will weep.
V, v, 135

He shall have a noble memory. *V, v, 155*

PERICLES [1608–1609]

See, where she comes apparell'd like the spring.
Act I, sc. i, l. 12

Few love to hear the sins they love to act. *I, i, 92*

The sad companion, dull-ey'd melancholy. *I, ii, 2*

Third Fisherman: . . . Master, I marvel how the fishes live
in the sea.
First Fisherman: Why, as men do a-land; the great ones
eat up the little ones. *II, i, 29*

CYMBELINE [1609–1610]

Lest the bargain should catch cold and starve.
Act I, sc. iv, l. 186

Hath his bellyful of fighting. *II, i, 24*

Hark! hark! the lark at heaven's gate sings,
And Phoebus 'gins arise,
His steeds to water at those springs
On chalic'd flowers that lies;
And winking Mary-buds begin
To ope their golden eyes:
With everything that pretty is,
My lady sweet, arise. *II, iii, 22*

As chaste as unsunn'd snow. *II, v, 13*

Some griefs are med'cinable. *III, ii, 33*

O! for a horse with wings! *III, ii, 49*

The game is up. *III, iii, 107*

Slander,
Whose edge is sharper than the sword, whose tongue
Outvenoms all the worms of Nile, whose breath
Rides on the posting winds and doth belie
All corners of the world. *III, iv, 35*

I have not slept one wink. *III, iv, 103*

Weariness
Can snore upon the flint when resty sloth
Finds the down pillow hard. *III, vi, 33*

An angel! or, if not,
An earthly paragon! *III, vi, 42*

Society is no comfort
To one not sociable. *IV, ii, 12*

I wear not
My dagger in my mouth. *IV, ii, 78*

Fear no more the heat o' the sun,
Nor the furious winter's rages;
Thou thy worldly task hast done,
Home art gone, and ta'en thy wages;
Golden lads and girls all must,
As chimney-sweepers, come to dust. *IV, ii, 258*

Quiet consummation have;
And renowned be thy grave! *IV, ii, 280*

Fortune brings in some boats that are not steer'd.
IV, iii, 46

Hang there like fruit, my soul,
Till the tree die! *V, v, 264*

SONNETS [1609]

From fairest creatures we desire increase,
That thereby beauty's rose might never die. *Sonnet 1, l. 1*

When forty winters shall besiege thy brow,
And dig deep trenches in thy beauty's field.

Sonnet 2, l. 1

Thou art thy mother's glass, and she in thee
Calls back the lovely April of her prime.

Sonnet 3, l. 9

Music to hear, why hear'st thou music sadly?
Sweets with sweet war not, joy delights in joy.

Sonnet 8, l. 1

Everything that grows
Holds in perfection but a little moment.   *Sonnet 15, l. 1*

Shall I compare thee to a summer's day?
Thou art more lovely and more temperate:
Rough winds do shake the darling buds of May,
And summer's lease hath all too short a date.

Sonnet 18, l. 1

But thy eternal summer shall not fade.

Sonnet 18, l. 9

The painful warrior famoused for fight,
After a thousand victories, once foil'd,
Is from the books of honor razed quite,
And all the rest forgot for which he toil'd.

Sonnet 25, l. 9

When in disgrace with fortune and men's eyes
I all alone beweep my outcast state,
And trouble deaf heaven with my bootless cries.

Sonnet 29, l. 1

Desiring this man's art, and that man's scope,
With what I most enjoy contented least;
Yet in these thoughts myself almost despising,
Haply I think on thee.   *Sonnet 29, l. 7*

For thy sweet love remember'd such wealth brings
That then I scorn to change my state with kings.

Sonnet 29, l. 13

When to the sessions of sweet silent thought
I summon up remembrance of things past,
I sigh the lack of many a thing I sought,
And with old woes new wail my dear times' waste.

Sonnet 30, l. 1

But if the while I think on thee, dear friend,
All losses are restor'd and sorrows end.   *Sonnet 30, l. 13*

Full many a glorious morning have I seen.   *Sonnet 33, l. 1*

Roses have thorns, and silver fountains mud;
Clouds and eclipses stain both moon and sun,
And loathsome canker lives in sweetest bud.
       All men make faults.   *Sonnet 35, l. 2*

Be thou the tenth Muse.   *Sonnet 38, l. 9*

For nimble thought can jump both sea and land.
                 Sonnet 44, l. 7

Against that time when thou shalt strangely pass,
And scarcely greet me with that sun, thine eye,
When love, converted from the thing it was,
Shall reasons find of settled gravity.   *Sonnet 49, l. 5*

Not marble, nor the gilded monuments
Of princes, shall outlive this powerful rime.
                 Sonnet 55, l. i.

Like as the waves make towards the pebbled shore,
So do our minutes hasten to their end.   *Sonnet 60, l. 1*

Time doth transfix the flourish set on youth
And delves the parallels in beauty's brow.   *Sonnet 60, l. 9*

When I have seen by Time's fell hand defaced
The rich proud cost of outworn buried age,
When sometime lofty towers I see down-rased
And brass eternal slave to mortal rage;
When I have seen the hungry ocean gain
Advantage on the kingdom of the shore,
And the firm soil win of the wat'ry main,
Increasing store with loss and loss with store.

Sonnet 64, l. 1

Ruin hath taught me thus to ruminate,
That Time will come and take my love away.
This thought is as a death, which cannot choose
But weep to have that which it fears to lose.

Sonnet 64, l. 11

Tir'd with all these, for restful death I cry. *Sonnet 66, l. 1*

And art made tongue-tied by authority. *Sonnet 66, l. 9*

And simple truth miscall'd simplicity,
And captive good attending captain ill. *Sonnet 66, l. 11*

No longer mourn for me when I am dead
Than you shall hear the surly sullen bell
Give warning to the world that I am fled
From this vile world, with vilest worms to dwell.

Sonnet 71, l. 1

That time of year thou mayst in me behold
When yellow leaves, or none, or few, do hang
Upon those boughs which shake against the cold,
Bare ruin'd choirs, where late the sweet
    birds sang. *Sonnet 73, l. 1*

Clean starved for a look. *Sonnet 75, l. 10*

Who is it that says most? which can say more
Than this rich praise, — that you alone are you?

Sonnet 84, l. 1

Farewell! thou art too dear for my possessing,
And like enough thou know'st thy estimate.

Sonnet 87, l. 1

In sleep a king, but, waking, no such matter.

Sonnet 87, l. 14

Ah! do not, when my heart hath 'scap'd this sorrow,
Come in the rearward of a conquer'd woe;
Give not a windy night a rainy morrow,
To linger out a purpos'd overthrow. *Sonnet 90, l. 5*

They that have power to hurt and will do none,
That do not do the thing they most do show,
Who, moving others, are themselves as stone,
Unmoved, cold, and to temptation slow. *Sonnet 94, l. 1*

They are the lords and owners of their faces,
Others but stewards of their excellence.
The summer's flower is to the summer sweet,
Though to itself it only live and die. *Sonnet 94, l. 7*

Lilies that fester smell far worse than weeds.
Sonnet 94, l. 14

The hardest knife ill-used doth lose his edge.
Sonnet 95, l. 14

How like a winter hath my absence been. *Sonnet 97, l. 1*

From you have I been absent in the spring,
When proud-pied April, dress'd in all his trim,
Hath put a spirit of youth in everything. *Sonnet 98, l. 1*

Sweets grown common lose their dear delight.
Sonnet 102, l. 12

To me, fair friend, you never can be old,
For as you were when first your eye I ey'd,
Such seems your beauty still. *Sonnet 104, l. 1*

When in the chronicle of wasted time
I see descriptions of the fairest wights,
And beauty making beautiful old rime,
In praise of ladies dead and lovely knights,
Then, in the blazon of sweet beauty's best,
Of hand, of foot, of lip, of eye, of brow,
I see their antique pen would have express'd
Even such a beauty as you master now. *Sonnet 106, l. 1*

Not mine own fears, nor the prophetic soul
Of the wide world dreaming on things to come,
Can yet the lease of my true love control,
Suppos'd as forfeit to a confin'd doom.
The mortal moon hath her eclipse endur'd,
And the sad augurs mock their own presage;
Incertainties now crown themselves assur'd,
And peace proclaims olives of endless age. *Sonnet 107, l. 1*

O! never say that I was false of heart,
Though absence seem'd my flame to qualify.
Sonnet 109, l. 1

That is my home of love: if I have rang'd,
Like him that travels, I return again. *Sonnet 109, l. 5*

Alas! 'tis true I have gone here and there,
And made myself a motley to the view,
Gor'd mine own thoughts,
sold cheap what is most dear,
Made old offenses of affections new. *Sonnet 110, l. 1*

My nature is subdu'd
To what it works in, like the dyer's hand. *Sonnet 111, l. 6*

Let me not to the marriage of true minds
Admit impediments. Love is not love
Which alters when it alteration finds,
Or bends with the remover to remove:
O, no! it is an ever-fixed mark,
That looks on tempests and is never shaken;
It is the star to every wandering bark,
Whose worth's unknown, although his height be taken.
Love's not Time's fool, though rosy lips and cheeks
Within his bending sickle's compass come;
Love alters not with his brief hours and weeks,
But bears it out even to the edge of doom.
If this be error, and upon me prov'd,
I never writ, nor no man ever lov'd. *Sonnet 116*

What potions have I drunk of Siren tears,
Distill'd from limbecks foul as hell within.

Sonnet 119, l. 1

O benefit of ill! *Sonnet 119, l. 9*

And ruin'd love, when it is built anew,
Grows fairer than at first, more strong, far greater.

Sonnet 119, l. 11

'Tis better to be vile than vile esteem'd,
When not to be receives reproach of being.

Sonnet 121, l. 1

The expense of spirit in a waste of shame
Is lust in action; and till action, lust
Is perjur'd, murderous, bloody, full of blame,
Savage, extreme, rude, cruel, not to trust;
Enjoy'd no sooner but despised straight;
Past reason hunted; and no sooner had,
Past reason hated, as a swallow'd bait,
On purpose laid to make the taker mad:
Mad in pursuit, and in possession so;
Had, having, and in quest to have, extreme;
A bliss in proof, — and prov'd, a very woe;
Before, a joy propos'd; behind, a dream.

All this the world well knows; yet none knows well
To shun the heaven that leads men to this hell.
Sonnet 129

My mistress' eyes are nothing like the sun;
Coral is far more red than her lips' red:
If snow be white, why then her breasts are dun;
If hairs be wires, black wires grow on her head.
Sonnet 130, l. 1

When my love swears that she is made of truth,
I do believe her, though I know she lies. *Sonnet 138, l. 1*

Two loves I have of comfort and despair,
Which like two spirits do suggest me still. *Sonnet 144, l. 1*

Poor soul, the center of my sinful earth. *Sonnet 146, l. 1*

So shalt thou feed on Death, that feeds on men,
And Death once dead, there's no more dying then.
Sonnet 146, l. 13

Past cure I am, now Reason is past care,
And frantic-mad with evermore unrest. *Sonnet 147, l. 9*

For I have sworn thee fair, and thought thee bright,
Who art as black as hell, as dark as night. *Sonnet 147, l. 13*

THE WINTER'S TALE [1610–1611]

You pay a great deal too dear for what's given freely.
Act I, sc. i, l. 18

Two lads that thought there was no more behind
But such a day tomorrow as today,
And to be boy eternal. *I, ii, 63*

We were as twinn'd lambs that did frisk i' the sun,
And bleat the one at the other: what we chang'd
Was innocence for innocence. *I, ii, 67*

Paddling palms and pinching fingers. *I, ii, 116*

Affection! thy intention stabs the center:
Thou dost make possible things not so held,
Communicat'st with dreams. *I, ii, 139*

He makes a July's day short as December. *I, ii, 169*

A sad tale's best for winter.
I have one of sprites and goblins. *II, i,* 24

The silence often of pure innocence
Persuades when speaking fails. *II, ii,* 41

It is a heretic that makes the fire,
Not she which burns in 't. *II, iii,* 115

I am a feather for each wind that blows. *II, iii,* 153

What's gone and what's past help
Should be past grief. *III, ii,* 223

Exit, pursued by a bear. *III, iii,* 57

This is fairy gold, boy, and 'twill prove so. *III, iii,* 127

Then comes in the sweet o' the year. *IV, ii,* 3

A snapper-up of unconsidered trifles. *IV, ii,* 26

For the life to come, I sleep out the thought of it.
IV, ii, 30

Jog on, jog on, the footpath way,
And merrily hent the stile-a:
A merry heart goes all the day,
Your sad tires in a mile-a. *IV, ii, 133*

For you there's rosemary and rue; these keep
Seeming and savor all the winter long. *IV, iii, 74*

Here's flowers for you:
Hot lavender, mints, savory, marjoram,
The marigold, that goes to bed wi' the sun,
And with him rises weeping: these are flowers
Of middle summer, and I think they are given
To men of middle age. *IV, iii, 103*

Daffodils,
That come before the swallow dares, and take
The winds of March with beauty. *IV, iii, 118*

What you do
Still betters what is done. *IV, iii, 135*

When you do dance, I wish you
A wave o' the sea, that you might ever do
Nothing but that. *IV, iii, 140*

Lawn as white as driven snow. *IV, iii,* 220

I love a ballad in print, a-life, for then we are sure they
are true. *IV, iii,* 262

The self-same sun that shines upon his court
Hides not his visage from our cottage, but
Looks on alike. *IV, iii,* 457

I'll queen it no inch further,
But milk my ewes and weep. *IV, iii,* 462

Prosperity's the very bond of love,
Whose fresh complexion and whose heart together
Affliction alters. *IV, iii,* 586

Let me have no lying; it becomes none but tradesmen.
IV, iii, 747

To purge melancholy. *IV, iii,* 792

There's time enough for that. *V, iii,* 128

THE TEMPEST [1611–1612]

He hath no drowning mark upon him; his complexion
is perfect gallows. *Act I, sc. i, l. 33*

Now would I give a thousand furlongs of sea for an
acre of barren ground. *I, i, 70*

I would fain die a dry death. *I, i, 73*

What seest thou else
In the dark backward and abysm of time? *I, ii, 49*

By telling of it,
Made such a sinner of his memory,
To credit his own lie. *I, ii, 100*

Your tale, sir, would cure deafness. *I, ii, 106*

My library
Was dukedom large enough. *I, ii, 109*

The very rats
Instinctively have quit it. *I, ii, 147*

Knowing I lov'd my books, he furnish'd me,
From mine own library with volumes that
        I prize above my dukedom. *I, ii, 166*

I [Ariel] will be correspondent to command,
    And do my spiriting gently. *I, ii, 297*

You taught me language; and my profit on 't
Is, I know how to curse: the red plague rid you,
    For learning me your language! *I, ii, 363*

        Come unto these yellow sands,
            And then take hands:
        Curtsied when you have, and kiss'd —
            The wild waves whist, —
        Foot it featly here and there. *I, ii, 375*

This music crept by me upon the waters,
Allaying both their fury, and my passion,
        With its sweet air. *I, ii, 389*

            Full fathom five thy father lies;
                Of his bones are coral made:
            Those are pearls that were his eyes:
                Nothing of him that doth fade,
                But doth suffer a sea-change
            Into something rich and strange. *I, ii, 394*

The fringed curtains of thine eye advance. *I, ii, 405*

Lest too light winning
Make the prize light. *I, ii, 448*

There's nothing ill can dwell in such a temple:
If the ill spirit have so fair a house,
Good things will strive to dwell with 't. *I, ii, 454*

He receives comfort like cold porridge. *II, i, 10*

I' the commonwealth I would by contraries
Execute all things; for no kind of traffic
Would I admit; no name of magistrate;
Letters should not be known; riches, poverty,
And use of service, none; contract, succession,
Bourn, bound of land, tilth, vineyard, none;
No use of metal, corn, or wine, or oil;
No occupation; all men idle, all;
And women too, but innocent and pure. *II, i, 154*

What's past is prologue. *II, i, 261*

Open-ey'd Conspiracy
His time doth take. *II, i, 309*

A very ancient and fish-like smell. *II, ii, 27*

Misery acquaints a man with strange bedfellows.
II, ii, 42

How cam'st thou to be the siege of this moon-calf?
II, ii, 115

I shall laugh myself to death. *II, ii, 167*

'Ban, 'Ban, Ca — Caliban,
Has a new master — Get a new man. *II, ii, 197*

For several virtues
Have I lik'd several women. *III, i, 42*

Ferdinand: . . . Here's my hand.
Miranda: And mine, with my heart in't. *III, i, 89*

Thou deboshed fish thou. *III, ii, 30*

Keep a good tongue in your head. *III, ii, 41*

Flout 'em, and scout 'em; and scout 'em, and flout 'em;
Thought is free. *III, ii, 133*

He that dies pays all debts. *III, ii, 143*

The isle is full of noises,
Sounds and sweet airs, that give delight, and hurt not.
Sometimes a thousand twangling instruments
Will hum about mine ears; and sometimes voices,
That, if I then had wak'd after long sleep,
Will make me sleep again. *III, ii, 146*

A kind
Of excellent dumb discourse. *III, iii, 38*

Do not give dalliance
Too much the rein. *IV, i, 51*

Our revels now are ended. These our actors,
As I foretold you, were all spirits and
Are melted into air, into thin air:
And, like the baseless fabric of this vision,
The cloud-capp'd towers, the gorgeous palaces,
The solemn temples, the great globe itself,
Yea, all which it inherit, shall dissolve
And, like this insubstantial pageant faded,

Leave not a rack behind. We are such stuff
As dreams are made on, and our little life
Is rounded with a sleep. *IV, i, 148*

With foreheads villainous low. *IV, i, 252*

But this rough magic
I here abjure. *V, i, 50*

I'll break my staff,
Bury it certain fathoms in the earth,
And, deeper than did ever plummet sound,
I'll drown my book. *V, i, 54*

Where the bee sucks, there suck I
In a cowslip's bell I lie;
There I couch when owls do cry.
On the bat's back I do fly
After summer merrily:
Merrily, merrily shall I live now
Under the blossom that hangs on the bough. *V, i, 88*

O brave new world,
That has such people in't! *V, i, 183*

Let us not burden our remembrances
With a heaviness that's gone. *V, i, 199*

This thing of darkness I
Acknowledge mine. *V, i, 274*

And my ending is despair,
Unless I be reliev'd by prayer,
Which pierces so that it assaults
Mercy itself and frees all faults. *Epilogue, l. 15*

KING HENRY THE EIGHTH [1613]

No man's pie is freed
From his ambitious finger. *Act I, sc. i, l. 52*

The force of his own merit makes his way. *I, i, 64*

Heat not a furnace for your foe so hot
That it do singe yourself. *I, i, 140*

If I chance to talk a little wild, forgive me;
I had it from my father. *I, iv, 26*

The mirror of all courtesy. *II, i, 53*

Go with me, like good angels, to my end;
And, as the long divorce of steel falls on me,
Make of your prayers one sweet sacrifice,
And lift my soul to heaven. *II, i, 75*

This bold bad man. *II, ii, 44*

'Tis better to be lowly born,
And range with humble livers in content,
Than to be perk'd up in a glist'ring grief
And wear a golden sorrow. *II, iii, 19*

I would not be a queen
For all the world. *II, iii, 45*

Orpheus with his lute made trees,
And the mountain-tops that freeze,
Bow themselves, when he did sing. *III, i, 3*

Heaven is above all yet; there sits a judge
That no king can corrupt. *III, i, 99*

'Tis well said again;
And 'tis a kind of good deed to say well:
And yet words are no deeds.   *III, ii, 153*

And then to breakfast with
What appetite you have.   *III, ii, 203*

I have touch'd the highest point of all my greatness;
And from that full meridian of my glory,
I haste now to my setting: I shall fall
Like a bright exhalation in the evening,
And no man see me more.   *III, ii, 224*

Press not a falling man too far.   *III, ii, 334*

Farewell! a long farewell, to all my greatness!
This is the state of man: today he puts forth
The tender leaves of hopes; tomorrow blossoms,
And bears his blushing honors thick upon him;
The third day comes a frost, a killing frost;
And, when he thinks, good easy man, full surely
His greatness is a-ripening, nips his root,
And then he falls, as I do. I have ventur'd,
Like little wanton boys that swim on bladders,
This many summers in a sea of glory,
But far beyond my depth: my high-blown pride
At length broke under me, and now has left me,

Weary and old with service, to the mercy
Of a rude stream, that must forever hide me.
Vain pomp and glory of this world, I hate ye:
I feel my heart new open'd. O! how wretched
Is that poor man that hangs on princes' favors!
There is, betwixt that smile we would aspire to,
That sweet aspect of princes, and their ruin,
More pangs and fears than wars or women have;
And when he falls, he falls like Lucifer,
Never to hope again. *III, ii,* 352

A peace above all earthly dignities,
A still and quiet conscience. *III, ii,* 380

A load would sink a navy. *III, ii,* 384

And sleep in dull cold marble. *III, ii,* 434

Cromwell, I charge thee, fling away ambition:
By that sin fell the angels. *III, ii,* 441

Love thyself last: cherish those hearts that hate thee;
Corruption wins not more than honesty.
Still in thy right hand carry gentle peace,
To silence envious tongues: be just, and fear not.
Let all the ends thou aim'st at be thy country's,

Thy God's, and truth's; then if thou fall'st, O Cromwell!
Thou fall'st a blessed martyr! *III, ii, 444*

Had I but serv'd my God with half the zeal
I serv'd my king, he would not in mine age
Have left me naked to mine enemies. *III, ii, 456*

An old man, broken with the storms of state,
Is come to lay his weary bones among ye;
Give him a little earth for charity. *IV, ii, 21*

He gave his honors to the world again,
His blessed part to heaven, and slept in peace. *IV, ii, 29*

So may he rest; his faults lie gently on him! *IV, ii, 31*

He was a man
Of an unbounded stomach. *IV, ii, 33*

Men's evil manners live in brass; their virtues
We write in water. *IV, ii, 45*

He was a scholar, and a ripe and good one;
Exceeding wise, fair-spoken, and persuading;
Lofty and sour to them that lov'd him not;

But, to those men that sought him sweet as
summer. *IV, ii, 51*

To dance attendance on their lordships' pleasures.
V, ii, 30

Nor shall this peace sleep with her; but as when
The bird of wonder dies, the maiden phoenix,
Her ashes new-create another heir
As great in admiration as herself. *V, v, 40*

Wherever the bright sun of heaven shall shine,
His honor and the greatness of his name
Shall be, and make new nations. *V, v, 51*

Some come to take their ease
And sleep an act or two. *Epilogue, l. 2*

SHAKESPEARE'S EPITAPH

Good friend, for Jesus' sake forbear
To dig the dust enclosed here;
Blest be the man that spares these stones,
And curst be he that moves my bones.